She turned to go, only half-heartedly, because he had moved in to kiss her—and not on the cheek.

One kiss couldn't hurt, Cate told herself. It was time to be kissed by someone else now, she decided as his mouth met hers.

Except she'd never known a kiss like it.

It was everything a kiss should be.

It was very slow and measured, his lips light at first, nudging hers into slow movement. His hands crept around her waist and his tongue slipped in and slid around hers, slowly, letting her acclimatise to the taste of him. And so easily she did. He tasted of raspberry and vodka and something else too, which Cate couldn't quite place.

He took things slowly, but not for long. Just as she started to relax—just as she thought she could manage a kiss goodbye with Juan—he breathed into her, shed a low moan into her, pressed into her, pushed in his tongue more deeply. And Cate found her missing ingredient then—it was a dash of sin that he tasted of…

Dear Reader,

As I wrote Juan and Cate's story it was never my intention to do two linked books. I adored Juan, and loved following his journey, but while I was speaking about my plot with my writing friend Fiona McArthur she said, 'I think you love Harry too.'

Is it possible to love two heroes at once?

Please don't think less of me, but my answer is YES!

They have both known tragedy, but in very different ways, and they both make me laugh. The funniest thing for me, while writing this, was that I discovered beauty really is in the eye of the beholder. Neither of my heroines remotely fancied the other's hero.

Their creator did, though! :)

I hope you enjoy their stories.

Happy reading!

Carol xxx

The second story in Carol Marinelli's
***Bayside Hospital Heartbreakers!* duet**

THE ACCIDENTAL ROMEO

is also available this month
from Mills & Boon® Medical Romance™

TEMPTED BY DR MORALES

BY
CAROL MARINELLI

Published in Great Britain 2014
by Mills & Boon, an imprint of Harlequin (UK) Limited,
Eton House, 18-24 Paradise Road, Richmond, Surrey, TW9 1SR

© 2014 Carol Marinelli

ISBN: 978 0 263 24362 8

Carol Marinelli recently filled in a form where she was asked for her job title and was thrilled, after all these years, to be able to put down her answer as 'writer'. Then it asked what Carol did for relaxation. After chewing her pen for a moment Carol put down the truth—'writing'. The third question asked—'What are your hobbies?' Well, not wanting to look obsessed or, worse still, boring, she crossed the fingers on her free hand and answered 'swimming and tennis'. But, given that the chlorine in the pool does terrible things to her highlights, and the closest she's got to a tennis racket in the last couple of years is watching the Australian Open, I'm sure you can guess the real answer!

Recent books by Carol Marinelli:

Mills & Boon® Medical Romance™

SECRETS OF A CAREER GIRL††
DR DARK AND FAR TOO DELICIOUS††
NYC ANGELS: REDEEMING THE PLAYBOY**
SYDNEY HARBOUR HOSPITAL:
  AVA'S RE-AWAKENING*
HERS FOR ONE NIGHT ONLY?
CORT MASON—DR DELECTABLE
HER LITTLE SECRET
ST PIRAN'S: RESCUING PREGNANT CINDERELLA†
KNIGHT ON THE CHILDREN'S WARD

**NYC Angels*
*Sydney Harbour Hospital
†St Piran's Hospital
††Secrets on the Emergency Wing*

Mills & Boon® Modern™ Romance

A LEGACY OF SECRETS‡
PLAYING THE DUTIFUL WIFE
BEHOLDEN TO THE THRONE~
BANISHED TO THE HAREM~
AN INDECENT PROPOSITION
A SHAMEFUL CONSEQUENCE
HEART OF THE DESERT
THE DEVIL WEARS KOLOVSKY

*~Empire of the Sands
‡Sicily's Coretti Dynasty*

**These books are also available in eBook format
from www.millsandboon.co.uk**

With love to Fiona McArthur
I love our chats
C xxx

Praise for
Carol Marinelli:

'A heartwarming story about taking a chance and not
letting the past destroy the future. It is strengthened by
two engaging lead characters and a satisfying ending.'
—*RT Book Reviews* on
THE LAST KOLOVSKY PLAYBOY

'Carol Marinelli writes with sensitivity,
compassion and understanding, and
ST PIRAN'S: RESCUING PREGNANT CINDERELLA
is not just a powerful romance but an uplifting
and inspirational tale about starting over,
new beginnings and moving on.'
—*CataRomance*

If you love Carol Marinelli,
you'll fall head over heels
for Carol's sparkling, touching, witty debut.

PUTTING ALICE BACK TOGETHER

available from MIRA® Books

CHAPTER ONE

'SORRY, JUAN, I didn't mean to wake you.' Cate Nicholls stopped twisting a long brown curl around her finger and cringed at the sound of Juan's deep, heavily accented—but clearly sleepy—voice when he answered the phone.

'It is no problem. Is that you, Cate?'

'Yes.' She blushed a little that Juan had recognised her voice. He had only done a few locum shifts at the Melbourne Bayside Hospital emergency department, but the tension between them sizzled. Cate had tried everyone she could think of before finally accepting Harry's suggestion and phoning Juan to see if he could come in. A fully qualified anaesthetist from Argentina, he was travelling around the world for a year or two and was as sexy-as-sin as a man could possibly be and still remain popular. 'I'm really sorry to have disturbed you. Were you working last night?'

'No.'

'Oh!' Cate glanced up at the clock—it was two p.m., why on earth would he still be in bed? Then Cate heard the sound of a female voice and cringed again as Juan told whoever the woman was that he took three sugars in his coffee. Then his silken voice returned to Cate.

'So, what can I do for you?'

'Sheldon called in sick and we haven't been able to get anyone else in to cover him.'

'Does Harry know that you're calling me?'

Cate laughed—Harry, one of the senior emergency department consultants, went into sulking mode whenever Juan was around; he was still annoyed that Juan had knocked back his offer of a three-month contract to work in the department. 'It was Harry who suggested that I call you.'

'So, what time do you want me to come in?'

'As soon as you can get here.' Cate looked out at the busy emergency department. 'It's really starting to fill up...' She paused for a moment as Harry said something. 'Could you hold on, please, Juan?' Cate called out to Harry, 'What did you say?'

'Tell Juan that even though we really need him to get here as soon as possible, he can stop for a haircut on the way if he feels so inclined!'

Juan's shaggy long black hair, unshaven appearance and relaxed dress sense drove Harry crazy and Cate was smiling as she got back to her conversation with Juan. 'I assume that you heard that?'

'I did,' Juan answered. 'Tell Harry that he loves me really.' Cate listened as Juan yawned and stretched and she tried not to think about him in bed, naked, at two in the afternoon. 'Okay,' he said. 'I'll just have a quick shower and I'll be there as soon as I can.'

'Thanks, Juan.' Cate hung up the phone and wrote his name on the board. Harry glanced over and gave a quick shake of his head.

'If ever there was a man inappropriately named, it's Dr Morales,' Harry said, and Cate had to laugh. Juan had quite a reputation, and even just writing his name down would have a few staff scurrying off to check their make-up and hair.

Cate refused to.

Washing her hands before heading back out to the patients, she saw her reflection in the mirror. Yes, her shoulder-length hair could do with being re-tied and her serious hazel eyes might look better with a slick of mascara, but she simply refused to make that effort for Juan.

She wasn't about to play with fire.

With three older brothers who had all been wild, to say the least, not a lot shocked the rather sensible Cate, but Juan managed to at times—either with his daredevil sports or with the endless women he briefly bedded. He raised more than a few eyebrows when he happily regaled his colleagues with tales of his trip around Australia, but what shocked Cate most was the internal fight she was having to put up to not simply give in to that sensual smile and dive headfirst into his bed.

They had hit the ground flirting but then Cate had backed off—soon realising that Juan and his rather reprobate ways were far more than she could handle.

Cate had returned from two weeks' annual leave, newly single after breaking up with her boyfriend of more than two years, and her stomach had turned over at the very sight of Juan. She'd never had such a violent reaction to anyone and, foolishly, she had told herself she was just testing out her flirting wings on the sexy locum, just indulging in a little play flirt the first time they had met.

Cate had never really thought he'd ask her to join him for a drink that night, though his eyes had said bed.

She still burnt at the memory of their first meeting—

the rush that had come as she'd met his grey eyes, the desire to say yes, to hell with it all, for once to give in and choose to be reckless. Instead, she had refused his offer politely and, in the few times she'd seen him since then, Cate had played things down—denied the attraction that sizzled between them and tried her best to keep things strictly about work.

'Juan is a very good doctor, though,' Cate reminded Harry, because even if Juan was a bit of a rake, there was no disputing that fact.

'Yes, but his talent's wasted,' Harry said, but then sighed. 'Maybe I'm just envious.'

'I've never met a more talented emergency doctor than you,' Cate said, and she meant it. Harry was a fantastic emergency doctor as well as a highly renowned hand surgeon, only it wasn't Juan's medical talent that Harry was referring to.

'I meant maybe I'm envious of Juan's freedom, his take-it-or-leave-it attitude. He actually doesn't give a damn what anyone thinks. It would be lovely just to work one or two shifts a week and spend the rest of the time kicking back!' Harry gave a wry smile. 'But, then, Juan doesn't have four-year-old twins to worry about. Make that, Juan doesn't have anything to worry about.'

'Are things not getting any better?' Cate asked. She liked Harry a lot and had been devastated for him when his wife had been brought in last year after a car crash. Jill had died two weeks later in ICU, leaving Harry a single father to his young twins, Charlotte and Adam.

'The nanny just handed in her notice,' Harry said. 'Another one!'

Cate gave a sympathetic groan but Harry just rolled

his eyes and headed back out to deal with the patients. 'It will sort itself out,' Harry said.

'Ooh!' Kelly smiled when she saw Juan's name up on the board. 'That just brightened up my afternoon! With a bit of luck Juan will come out for drinks with us tonight after work.' Kelly winked.

'I'm sure that he will,' Cate said. 'I can't make it, though.'

'Come on, Cate,' Kelly pushed. 'You said that you would. It's Friday night, you can't sit around moping about Paul…'

'I'm not moping about Paul. When I said that I'd come out, I didn't realise that I was working in the morning,' Cate lied.

'But you said that you'd drive,' Kelly reminded her. 'It's still a week till payday.'

Yes, Cate thought, she had said she'd drive but that had been before she had known Juan would be working into the evening—he wasn't exactly known for turning down a night out.

Juan worked to live rather than lived to work—that had been his explanation when he had irked Harry by turning down his job offer. Juan had told Harry that he would prefer to work casual shifts at various Melbourne hospitals rather than be tied to one place. And, given he only worked one or two shifts a week, it had been thanks but, no, thanks from Juan. Cate had been surprised that Harry had even offered him the role.

He was, though, an amazing doctor.

He was amazing, Cate conceded to herself as she went to help Kelly make up some fresh gurneys and do a quick tidy of the cubicles.

Juan was also the last complication she needed.

Still, she put his impending arrival out of her mind, just glad to have the doctor shortage under control for now.

'Where's Christine?' Cate asked as she stripped a gurney and gave it a wipe down before making it up with fresh linen.

'Guess,' Kelly answered. 'She's hiding in her office. If you do get the job, please don't let that ever be you!'

Cate was soon to be interviewed for the role of nurse unit manager and it was fairly certain that the position would be hers. Lillian, the director of acute nursing, had practically told her so. Cate was already more hands on with the patients than most of the associate nurse unit managers, and if she did get the role she had no intention of hiding herself away in the office or going over the stock orders to try and save a bean. It had also been heavily hinted that, after Christine's haphazard brand of leadership, the powers that be wanted a lot more order in Emergency—and it had been none-too-subtly pointed out that the nurses were not there to babysit Harry's twins.

If she did get the job, Cate knew there was going to be a lot to deal with.

'Is this cubicle ready?' Abby, who was doing triage, popped her head in. 'I've got a gentleman that needs to be seen.'

'Bring him in,' Cate said. 'Kelly, if you could carry on sorting out any empty cubicles, that would be great.'

Kelly nodded and headed off and Cate took the handover as they helped the painfully thin gentleman move from the wheelchair to the gurney. His wife watched anxiously.

'This is Reece Anderson,' Abby introduced. 'He's

thirty-four years old and has recently completed a course of chemotherapy for a melanoma on his left thigh. Reece has had increasing nausea since this morning as well as abdominal pain.'

'He didn't tell me he was in pain till lunchtime.' There was an edge to his wife's voice. 'I thought the vomiting was the after effects of the chemo.'

'Okay, Reece.' Cate introduced herself. 'I'm going to help you to get into a gown and take some observations and then we shall get you seen just as soon as we can.' Reece was clearly very uncomfortable as well as dehydrated, and there was also considerable tension between him and his wife.

'The heat has made this last round of treatment unbearable,' his wife said. 'We don't have air-conditioning.' She looked more tense than the patient. 'I'm Amanda, by the way.'

'Hi, Amanda. Yes, I'm sure the heat isn't helping,' Cate said as she looked at Reece's dry lips and felt his skin turgor. 'We'll get a drip started soon.'

Melbourne was in the grip of a prolonged heat wave and more patients than usual were presenting as dehydrated. Cate had been moaning about the heat and lack of sleep herself, but to imagine being unwell and going through chemotherapy made her rethink her grumbles.

'Why don't you go home?' Reece suggested to his wife as, between retches, Cate helped him undress. 'I could be here for ages.'

'I've told you, I'm not going home. I don't want to leave you till I know what's happening.' Amanda's response was terse.

'You have to pick up the kids from school.'

'I'm going to ring Stella and let her know what's going on. She can get them…'

'Just go home, will you?' Reece snapped.

Cate looked over at Amanda and saw that she was close to tears.

'Just leave,' Reece said.

'Oh, I might just do that!' Amanda's voice held a challenge and Cate guessed this wasn't the first time they'd had this row. 'I'm going to ring Stella and ask her to pick them up.'

Amanda walked out of the cubicle and Reece rested back on the pillows as Cate took his baseline observations. 'I can't believe I'm back in hospital. Amanda should be sorting out the children, not me.'

Cate didn't comment; instead, she headed out and had a brief word with Harry, who was working with Kelly on a critical patient who had just arrived. He said he would get there just as soon as he could but, given how long the wait might be, Harry asked if Cate could take some bloods and start an IV.

Reece was pretty uncommunicative throughout but, as she went to leave, finally he asked a question. 'Do you think it's the cancer spreading?'

'I think it's far too early to be speculating about anything,' Cate said. 'We'll get these bloods off and a doctor will be in just as soon as possible.'

While she had sympathy for Reece and could guess how scared he must be, Cate's heart went out to Amanda when she found her crying by the vending machine.

'Come in here,' Cate offered, opening up an interview room to give Amanda some privacy. The interview rooms were beyond dreary, painted brown and with hard seats and a plastic table, but at least they were private. 'I know you must be very worried but it's far too early to know what's going on.'

'I can deal with whatever's going on health-wise,' Amanda said. 'We've been dealing with it for months now. It's Reece that I can't handle—his moods and constantly telling me to leave him alone.'

'It must be terribly hard,' Cate offered, wishing she could say more.

'It's nearly impossible.' Amanda shook her head with hopelessness. 'I'm starting to think that maybe he really doesn't want me around.'

'I doubt that,' Cate replied.

'So do I.' Amanda took a drink of coffee and slowly started to calm down—all she had needed was a short reprieve. 'You know, if that really is what he wants, then tough! I'm not going to walk away,' Amanda said, draining her drink and screwing up the cup as she threw it into the bin. 'Like it or not, I'm not going anywhere.' Amanda wiped her eyes and blew her nose then walked back to be with her husband.

Cate was wondering if she should try and find the intern to see Reece, though she did want someone more senior; then she considered calling in a favour from one of the surgical team and asking them to come down without an emergency doctor's referral, but then she saw Juan walk in.

He really was the most striking man Cate had ever seen. His tall, muscular frame was enhanced by the black Cuban-heeled boots that he wore. Today he was wearing black jeans with a heavily buckled belt and a grey and black shirt that was crumpled. His black hair was long enough that it could easily be tied back, but instead it fell onto his broad shoulders and, fresh from the shower, his hair left a slight damp patch on his shirt.

Cate's first thought on seeing him wasn't relief that finally there was an extra pair of hands and she could get Reece seen quickly.

Instead, as always, he begged the question—how on earth did she manage to say no to that? He was sex on long legs certainly, but more than that he made her smile, made her laugh. Juan just changed the whole dynamics of the place.

'You made good time!' Cate said, as he came over and she caught the heady whiff of Juan fresh from the shower.

'I got a lift.'

Ah, yes, Cate reminded herself, he'd had company when she'd called. Juan didn't have a car, he wasn't in any one place long enough for that, so instead he used public transport or, more often than not, he ran to work and treated everyone to the delicious sight of him breathless and sweaty before he headed for the staff shower.

'Where would you like me to start?' he asked. Juan was always ready to jump straight into work.

'Cubicle four,' Cate said, giving him a brief background on the way. She saw Reece's and Amanda's eyes widen just a fraction as a very foreign, rather unconventional-looking doctor entered the cubicle, yet Juan was so good with patients that within a moment he had Reece at ease.

Juan put one long, booted foot on the lower frame of the gurney and leant in and chatted with Reece about his medical history and symptoms before standing up straight.

'Can I borrow your stethoscope?' he asked Cate.

'There's one on the wall,' Cate said. There usually wasn't but the rather meticulous Cate had prepared the cubicle herself.

'I can't hear very well with them,' Juan said. 'I prefer yours.'

'I know! You took it home with you last time you *borrowed* it.'

'I brought it back,' he pointed out, but he took down one of the cheap hospital-issue ones and started listening to Reece's chest.

He cursed in Spanish and even Reece gave a small smile. 'They are useless. I should have brought mine but you said it was so busy that I was rushing to get here...' He winked at his patient and then Juan's full lips twitched into a small smile of triumph as Cate handed over her stethoscope.

'That's better,' Juan said.

Reece was soon back to feeling miserable as Juan examined him. He reduced Amanda to tears again when she tried to answer a question for him. 'I can speak for myself.'

'Okay,' Juan said, 'I am going lay you down and examine your stomach.' He turned and smiled at Amanda. 'Could you excuse us, please?'

Juan carefully examined his patient's abdomen as Reece tried to hide his grimaces.

'Reece...' Juan looked down. 'How long have you been sitting on this?'

'Since this morning.'

'Reece?' The doubt was obvious in Juan's voice.

'Last night…' Juan raised his eyebrows but said nothing, simply waited until Reece changed his story again. 'I woke up in pain the night before.'

'Is that one true?' Juan checked, and Reece nodded. 'Okay, I have to do a rectal examination.' As Cate helped Reece roll to his side, he was weary and close to crying. 'I'm sorry, Reece,' Juan said. 'I know it must be awful. It won't take long.'

He was so good with the patients. He never told them not to feel embarrassed, or that he'd done it a thousand times before; he just quickly examined him and as Reece was rolled onto his back again, Juan thanked him for his co-operation.

'Good man,' he said, and Reece nodded.

'What do you think is going on?' Reece asked, and this was where Juan was different from most doctors. This was where he was clearly senior because he gave Reece his tentative diagnosis.

'Your history makes things more complicated, of course…' Juan said. 'But I think you have appendicitis. I am going to ring the surgeons and get you seen as a priority.'

'Can I have something for the pain?'

'They don't like to give analgesia without first seeing the patient for themselves so they can get a clear picture.' Juan repeated what Cate had heard many times before, but again he showed just how experienced and confident he was as he continued speaking. 'Still, I will try bribing them by ordering a quick ultrasound while we wait for the bloods to come back. Hopefully I can give you something for the pain.'

It was still incredibly busy out in the department. Juan rang the surgeons and had a long discussion, then as he wrote up some analgesia he rang and arranged an ultrasound.

'Give Reece this for the pain and vomiting,' Juan said. 'I'll ring the lab and get the bloods pushed through. If we can get him round now for an ultrasound, the surgeons should be here by the time he comes back.'

'Sure.' Cate sorted out the drugs and then rang Christine and told her that she was taking a patient for an ultrasound and would she please come out of her office and work on the floor.

'That will go down well,' Kelly commented, picking up the constantly ringing phone.

'Do you know what?' Cate answered. 'I really don't care.'

Kelly held out the phone for Juan. 'A call for you.' He went to take it. 'Martina,' Kelly added.

Both women shared a look as he said a few terse words in Spanish and then promptly hung up. 'I spoke with Christine.' Juan looked at Cate. 'Did she not pass it on?'

'Pass what on?'

'I have had to speak to the nursing managers at the other hospitals where I work. Could you ask the nursing and reception staff not to put through certain personal calls for me?'

'Certain?' Cate checked.

'From Martina.'

'But if it's your mum or the girl you met last night...' Cate tried to keep the edge from her voice, but she felt like a secretary running his little black book when Juan was on call—women were ringing all the time '…then we're to put them through?'

'Okay, for *all* personal calls, just ask the staff to say they are not sure if Juan is working and that you'll take a message and leave it for him. I am just asking if the staff can be a bit more discreet.'

'The staff are discreet, Juan, but there's a difference between being discreet and rude. When it's clearly a personal call…' She took a breath. 'Fine, I'll speak to everyone.'

Juan got back to his notes and did not look up. It would simply open up a can of worms if he explained things.

He didn't want to explain things.

That was the reason he was travelling after all, no need for explanations, no past, no rules—just fun. Except Cate didn't want fun. She'd made that clear, even if not quite from the start.

He was going to do this shift and then go home.

Juan had just over two weeks to go in the country.

Had Cate said yes when he'd first asked her out they could have had an amazing few months.

Instead, she had made it very clear she wasn't interested in a brief fling with him.

She was interested, though.

Juan could feel it, he could smell it, he could almost taste it, but Cate refused to give in to it.

He wasn't going to try again.

Cate was a serious thing, a curious thing, and she was quietly driving him insane.

'Are you coming out for drinks tonight, Juan?' Kelly asked.

'Not tonight,' Juan said, and he heard Cate's small exhalation of relief.

Oh, well, Juan thought as he carried on writing up his notes.

She could relax soon.

He'd be gone.

CHAPTER TWO

'HOW ARE THINGS?' Juan came in to speak with Reece soon after he came back from ultrasound. The surgeons had examined him there and had ordered antibiotics and changed his IV regime, and Reece was now being prepared rapidly for Theatre.

'You tell me,' Reece said. 'They said that appendicitis was serious in someone with my immune system.'

'That's why they're starting you on all these antibiotics. We need to get you up to Theatre before it perforates,' Juan said.

'I shouldn't have left it,' Reece said. 'I thought it was cancer.'

'Of course you did,' Juan said, 'but it is an appendix flare-up nevertheless. I had a pregnant woman just last week...' He didn't continue, there was a lot to be done.

Cate was trying to sort out the antibiotics that the surgeons wanted. It had been incredibly tense during his ultrasound, Reece telling Amanda over and over that she should just go home. Cate had, on her way back from Ultrasound, suggested that Amanda wait in the interview room, just to have a break from the snipes from her husband.

'Cate, can I see Reece's IV regime?' Juan asked,

and then spoke to the patient. 'Though you need to be operated on, I want you to have a bolus of fluids before you go up.'

He was so direct he overrode the surgeons' IV regime with a stroke of his pen.

Juan saw Cate's rapid blink—not many people would have changed Jeff Henderson's plan. 'I just spoke to him and discussed some changes,' Juan said. 'Reece needs to be better hydrated before he's operated on.'

'I bet that went down well,' Cate said, repeating Kelly's sentiment from a little while ago.

'Jeff was fine.' Juan shrugged. 'And, like you, I really don't care if I offend at times. This is better for the patient.'

He handed over the chart and then spoke to Reece. 'I'm going to put another IV in you so that we can push fluids in and then I shall speak with your wife.'

'Can you tell her that there's no point hanging around?'

'She's not going to want to go home while you're in Theatre,' Cate pointed out as she added the medication to the flask.

'I just don't want her here,' Reece snapped. 'I don't want to be a burden.'

'Then stop being one,' Cate said, and Juan's head jerked up from the IV he was putting in. He'd heard a lot of straight talking—emergency nurses were very good at it—but hearing what Cate had to say to Reece made him falter momentarily.

'The illness and the treatment you are on must be awful, for *both* of you,' Cate continued to Reece, 'but I can think of nothing worse than loving someone who is sick and being repeatedly told that they don't want you there, that you'd be better off without them.'

'I think she'd be happier—' Reece attempted, but Cate didn't let him finish.

'I'm quite sure Amanda would be happier if you graciously accepted her love and affection and her need to take care of you, to help you *both* get through this.'

Juan headed over to the sharps box. He could feel his pulse pounding in his temples, feel the roar of blood in his ears, and, for reasons of his own, he wished he hadn't heard that, yet he felt compelled to respond.

'She's right.' Juan's voice was husky and he cleared his throat before continuing. 'Cate is right, Reece. If your wife didn't want to be here for you then she'd have gone long ago.'

'You don't know that.'

'Cate…' Juan turned '…could you go and speak with Amanda and let her know what is happening and then bring her in?'

'Sure,' Cate answered. 'Reece, are you okay with me letting her know that you have appendicitis?'

Reece nodded. Clearly Cate's words had had an impact on him because he let out a sigh and lay back on his pillows, but as she walked out of the cubicle he met suddenly serious grey eyes. Only then did Reece realise that there was more to come.

'Right,' Juan said to his patient. 'While we've got a moment, I'll tell you *exactly* what I do know.'

By the time Cate returned from taking Reece to Theatre, the critically injured patient had been moved as well and the place was settling down. All the staff worked hard to clear the backlog and at six Juan looked up at the clock and spoke to Harry.

'Why don't you go home?'

She saw Harry hesitate. There were other doctors on but no one particularly senior.

Except the locum just happened to be Juan.

'Go and have dinner with your children,' Juan said. 'I'm sure we'll cope.'

Juan would more than cope.

Everyone knew it.

'You're sure?' Harry checked. 'Dr Vermont won't get here till ten.'

'Of course,' Juan said. 'Anyway, the nightclubs don't really get going till midnight.'

Harry gave a wry smile and headed for home, and Cate did her best to avoid the six feet three of testosterone who sat and worked his way through a huge bunch of grapes between seeing patients.

Relieved that Juan wouldn't be joining them on their night out, Cate had relented and agreed to drive her friends, but before she headed off to get ready she did have a question for Juan. He was sitting writing up his notes before handing over to Dr Vermont.

'What did you say to Reece?'

'Reece?'

'The appendicitis.'

'I'm not with you,' Juan said, still writing his notes.

'He was a whole lot nicer to Amanda when we came back in. He even thanked her for being there for him when I took him up to Theatre.'

'He must have listened to what you said to him.' Juan shrugged and Cate walked off with a slight frown. Yes, she had been direct while talking to Reece but *something* had happened while she'd been speaking with Amanda. She was sure of it, because they had returned to a very different man—and Cate was positive Juan had had something to do with it.

She just had no idea what.

The night staff came on duty and Cate handed over the patients, then headed to the changing rooms, where there was a fight for the mirror.

'I thought Christine was coming?' Kelly said. 'She said she was a little while ago.'

'No.' Abby laughed. 'When she found out Juan wasn't coming, Christine changed her mind, of course. He's made it obvious that he's no longer interested—you'd think that she'd have taken the hint by now.'

Cate changed quickly, moaning that her strapless bra dug in and gave her four breasts before pulling on a black halterneck she had bought the previous weekend.

'Is that new?' Kelly asked as Cate pulled on a pale lilac skirt.

'Yep.' Cate smiled. 'And so are these!' She held up the most gorgeous pair of wedges—they were nothing like her usual choice, and had been an absolute impulse buy.

Her first.

Cate did up the straps around her ankles and blinked back sudden tears. She was still in that wobbly post-break-up stage, still trying to work out what had gone wrong, what *was* wrong.

She'd been happy with Paul, just not happy enough. She had loved him in so many ways, but she still hadn't been able to give Paul the answer he wanted. The answer everyone wanted! Her parents had been equally shocked when the rather predictable Cate had made a rather unpredictable choice.

Why had she ended it?

'Because...' had been her paltry response.

Even Cate didn't really know why.

Juan tried not to notice when the late staff all emerged from the changing rooms, changed and scented, like a noisy flock of butterflies floating down the corridor—but there was only one who drew the eye.

She had make-up on, not much just enough to accentuate her wary eyes, and her mouth should not be allowed out, unescorted by him, when it shimmered with gloss. A lilac skirt showed off her tanned legs and he did his best not to notice, as they walked past the nurses' station, her back, which was revealed in a halterneck.

'I'm not staying long,' he heard Cate warning her friends as they said goodbye and headed out. 'I've got to be back here in ten hours.'

'Are you sure you won't change your mind, Juan?' Kelly called over her shoulder.

And he should leave well alone. Cate wasn't, Juan guessed, up to what he had in mind.

Except he couldn't get her out of his head!

Her words to Reece had lowered his defences, and the scent of her as she walked past, the sight of her bare skin...it was surely worth one more shot?

Juan wanted their time.

'I might see you there,' Juan called out to the departing group, and watched her bare shoulders stiffen, watched as she very deliberately didn't turn round.

As she, still, denied him.

CHAPTER THREE

THE BAR WAS hot and crowded but it was equally hot outside; there was just no escaping the heat.

There was no escaping Juan.

She was terribly aware of him when, about an hour after they'd got there, he arrived.

He came over and bought everyone drinks, but Cate told him that she was happy with her soda water.

'When are you working with us again, Juan?' Abby shouted above the noise.

'I don't think I am,' Juan said. 'I have some shifts already booked in the city.'

'So this is your leaving do!' Kelly said.

'It might be...'

Cate stood there, watching her friends get louder, flirtier and more morose as they realised they might never see him again. By midnight, the night had turned into Juan Morales's unofficial send-off. So much so that there was now going to be an impromptu party back at his home.

Impromptu might just as well be his middle name, Cate thought as everyone asked her to come along.

'I'm working tomorrow!' Cate said it three times, not that anyone listened.

'It will be fun,' Abby insisted. 'Everyone's going back.'

Half the bar, it would seem, was lined up outside to take taxis to Juan's as, sober, fed up, tired and with her strapless bra digging into her, Cate headed out to her car.

'Thank you for this,' Juan said as he lowered himself into the passenger seat, far too tall for her rather small car. 'I really should get there first to let people in.'

'It's no problem.' Cate gave a slightly forced smile and then tried to turn it into a friendlier one as a couple of her colleagues and friends climbed into the back seat.

'You don't mind giving us a lift, do you, Cate?' Kelly checked, though not until she'd put her seat belt on.

'Of course not,' Cate said, and put the air conditioner on. The blast of cold air was especially welcome a moment later when Juan said, 'Cate, if you want to have a drink, you are very welcome to stay the night.'

Stay!

At Juan Morales's apartment for the night!

Cate turned and gave him the most incredulous smile she could muster, before starting the engine. 'Don't they have taxis in Argentina, Juan?'

He gave her a shameless smile back and then answered with his deep, heavily accented voice, which had Cate's stomach flip over on itself. 'I'm just letting you know that the offer is there.'

The offer had been there for a while now.

'I'm working at seven tomorrow morning.'

'You're staying for a drink, though,' Juan checked, but Cate answered him with a question of her own.

'Can you give me directions?' she said as she pulled out of the car park.

'Left ahead and then you go down...' He even managed to give a sexual connotation to the simplest directions, Cate thought, or was it that she was just incredibly aware of him sitting next to her?

Cate glanced over and caught a glimpse of his strong profile. His grey eyes were framed by dark lashes, his nose was straight and he had full lips that smiled easily. There was an exotic streak that seemed to run through every inch of him.

'Have you had your interview?' Juan asked.

'Not yet,' Cate said, surprised that he'd remembered. 'There are some external applications as well that they're going through.'

'So you would be the unit manager if you get it?'

'The nurse unit manager,' Cate corrected as she sat waiting for the traffic lights to change.

'Wouldn't you miss working with the patients?'

'I'd still be working with the patients,' came Cate's rather tart response, not that Juan seemed to notice the nerve he had just jarred, or, if he had, he chose to pursue it.

'Christine doesn't.'

She turned and met eyes that were more than happy to meet and hold hers. 'I'm not Christine,' Cate said, because rumour had it he'd been sleeping with Christine when he'd first arrived and Cate could well believe it. When Cate had come back from annual leave, she'd found Christine in floods of tears in the changing room and it hadn't been hard to work out why.

'No,' Juan said slowly and with a tinge of regret that made her throat tighten at the implication. His next loaded sentence seemed to insist she acknowledge the denied desire that simmered between them. 'You're not Christine.'

'The lights have changed,' Kelly called from the back.

As the car moved off Juan fiddled with her sound system and Cate cringed in embarrassment as a rather tragic break-up song came on.

'You should be listening to happier music,' Juan commented. 'All that will do is make you feel more miserable.'

'I'm not miserable at all.'

'Have you spoken to Paul since the break-up?' Abby chimed in from the back seat.

'Of course I have,' Cate said. 'It's all civil.'

'Which means that it was long overdue,' Juan commented, and Cate pursed her lips. It was the problem with being the so-called designated driver—you had to listen as things were discussed that generally wouldn't be.

'It doesn't have to be all smashing plates and tears,' Cate said, but didn't elaborate. Trust Juan to hit the nail on the head, though. Paul had been upset and uncomprehending at first, yet she had been calm and matter-of-fact once her decision to end it had been made.

Oh, she'd waited for the tears, for torrents of emotion to invade, for all the drama that seemed a necessary part of a relationship break-up to arrive—but they hadn't. She'd sat in her garden, sipping wine with her neighbour, Bridgette, with more a sense of relief than regret.

Juan was right, the break-up had been overdue.

'How much longer are you in Australia?' Kelly asked, and Juan turned a bit in his seat to answer and to chat with the girls in the back.

'Just over two weeks.'

'You should stay longer,' Kelly said.

'I can't,' Juan said, 'my visa expires the day after I leave.'

'Would you, though, if you could?' Kelly persisted.

'I think it's maybe time to move on.'

'Where now?' Cate asked, and Juan turned back to face the front.

'Turn right along the beach road and my place is about halfway.'

As she turned, the car jolted and Cate frowned. The car was not responding as it usually did, she could feel the groan of the engine.

'There's something wrong with the car,' Cate said, having appalling visions of breaking down a few metres from Juan's and, yes, ending up staying the night. The complication of a fling with Juan was something Cate did not need and frantically she looked at the dashboard. 'It's in manual…' Cate frowned but Juan had already worked it out—their hands met at the gearstick and Cate pulled hers away.

'My fault,' Juan said, 'my legs are too long.' He slotted it back into drive. 'My knees must have knocked the gearstick.'

God, he was potent. Cate's fingers were still tingling from the brief touch as she pulled up at his apartment. 'You are coming in?' Juan checked as she sat with the engine idling and there was a moment when she wanted to be the taxi martyr and drive off—but rather more than that, yes, she wanted a further glimpse of his world.

'Sure.'

Juan let them all in and it wasn't quite what Cate had

been expecting—it was a furnished rental apartment but a rather luxurious one with stunning beach views and a huge decking area outside. It was everything the well-heeled traveller needed for a few weeks of fun, Cate thought. Yet, despite the expensive furnishings and appliances, there was an emptiness and sparseness to it—a blandness even, broken only by his belongings.

Temporary.

Like Juan.

'This is the type of music you should be listening to,' Juan said, slotting his phone into some speakers. The room filled with music that under different circumstances Cate might want to dance to. Taxis were starting to arrive and, as more hospital personnel filled his home, Juan opened the French doors so that people could party inside or out, and then went to sort out drinks.

'What do you want, Cate?'

He made no secret that his interest was in her.

'I'll get something in a moment,' Cate said, and asked if she could use the bathroom.

'Straight down the hall,' Juan said. 'And to your left.'

She followed his directions but straight down the hall was his bedroom—the door was open, the bed rumpled and unmade, and for a wild, reckless moment she wanted to give in to his undeniable charm, could almost envision them tumbling on the bed, a knot of arms and legs.

Cate pushed open the bathroom door and let out a breath.

This wasn't like her at all.

She hadn't ever really envisioned herself that way with anyone, not even Paul. Bloody Juan had her head

going in directions it wasn't used to. A part of her
wanted to stop being sensible, ordered Cate and just
give in to the feelings he ignited—to be a little wild and
reckless for once. She knew that she was sending him
mixed messages, that at times she found herself flirting with him in a way she never had with anybody else.

Cate washed her hands and had to dry them on her
top because, of course, he didn't have hand towels, just
a wet beach towel hanging over the shower.

Whoops, there went her mind again, imagining that
huge body naked on the other side of the glass shower
door.

'Go home, Cate,' she said to herself. She was about
to do just that, but when she got back to the lounge Juan
handed her a large glass filled with ice and some dan-
gerous-looking cocktail.

'I'm driving,' Cate reminded him.

'I know, so I take care to make you something nice—
it is right to take care of the designated driver.'

It was fruity, refreshing and delicious, yet she didn't
want to be singled out for the Juan special treatment,
didn't want to be the latest caught in his spotlight, but
she knew that she was.

Cate danced a little, chatted with her friends, finished her drink and, having stayed a suitable length of
time, when she saw that he was safely speaking with
others, she said goodnight to Kelly.

'Stay for a bit longer,' Kelly pushed.

'I'm going to go.' Cate shook her head and slipped
quietly away and headed out to her car.

He really had chosen a lovely spot to live—there were
views of the bay to the front and behind was hillside. It
all looked so peaceful, it was hard to imagine that across

Victoria bush fires were raging, Cate thought, dragging in a breath of the warm, sultry night as she went into her bag for her keys.

'Cate.'

She jumped a little when she heard Juan call her name. Had she not lingered that second she would have been safely in her car; instead, she had no choice but to turn to him.

'Where I come from…' he walked slowly towards her, his boots crunching on the gravel '…you thank your host and say goodbye…'

'I didn't know you were such a stickler for convention.'

'I'm not,' Juan admitted, still walking towards her as she backed herself against the car. 'Just when it suits me.'

'Thank you for a lovely night.'

'And in my country,' Juan continued, 'the host would try to persuade you to stay for one more drink, would be offended that you were leaving so soon…' It was all very casual, except his hand had moved to her cheek and was moving a lock of her hair behind her ear.

'I'm good at offending people,' Cate said. 'There really is no need to take it personally.'

'Don't go.' He smiled. 'I only asked everyone back to get you here.'

She laughed.

She doubted it.

Actually, no, she didn't, she believed it. Anything was possible with Juan.

'I might not be called in to work again,' he said. 'So this could be it.'

'It could be.'

'I'd have liked to get to know you some more.'

She gave him a half-smile, but it wavered. Cate wanted to get to know him some more too, but for what? He made no secret that in a couple of weeks he would be gone. Juan seemed completely at ease with a brief fling, whereas it just wasn't in her nature.

Except, yes, she wanted more of Juan.

'Stay.'

'Juan…' Cate just couldn't do it and she tried to make a joke. 'I've got three brothers and they've all warned me about guys like you.'

'What?' He frowned.

'Come on, Juan.' She loathed how indecent he was. 'Won't whoever you were in bed with this afternoon mind?'

'What?' he asked again as the frown remained, but then it turned into a wicked smile. 'That was my cleaning lady,' he said. 'I fell asleep on the couch, watching daytime soaps.' He looked down at her, realised fully then that he hadn't had sex since he'd dumped Christine, since a certain Cate Nicholls had stepped into his life—how with one turn of his head he'd been very turned on. 'I love daytime soaps in Australia,' he said. 'They are filthy.'

Cate let out a small laugh.

She wasn't sure she believed him about the cleaning lady, but did it matter?

She wasn't his mother.

She wasn't anything and, yes, very soon he'd be gone.

She turned to go, only half-heartedly because he had moved in to kiss her, and not on the cheek.

One kiss couldn't hurt, Cate told herself.

It was time to have kissed someone else by now, Cate decided as his mouth met hers. Except she'd never known a kiss like it.

It was everything a kiss should be.

It was very slow and measured, his lips light on hers at first, nudging hers into slow movement. His hands crept around her waist and his tongue slipped in and slid around hers, slowly at first, letting her acclimatise herself to the taste of him, and she did, so easily. He tasted of raspberry and vodka and something else too, which Cate couldn't quite place.

He took things slowly, but not for long. Just as she started to relax, just as she thought she could manage a kiss goodbye with Juan, he breathed into her, shed a low moan into her, pressed into her, pushed in his tongue more deeply, and Cate found her missing ingredient—it was a dash of sin that he tasted of, because no kiss had turned her on so much. The press of his erection made her push her mound into him, the feel of his hot hand on her back had her skin turn to fire.

It wasn't just her first kiss after Paul, it was the first kiss she'd ever had that could propel her straight to the bedroom. She was kissing him back and with passion; it was still a slow kiss but their tongues danced with suggestion. His hand moved to her breast and how she wished she wasn't wearing a bra that was too tight and digging in, but a moment later she wasn't—as easily as that, Juan had undone it. Cate let out a small sigh of relief as her breast fell into his palm and then a moan of bliss as his hand cupped her and stroked.

'I want you…' He was at her neck and trailing his mouth down, she was stone-cold sober, yet almost top-less and drunk on lust. He kissed back up to her mouth and she could feel the trail of wetness he had left on her chest—and how she wanted him. Her hands moved to his head and she felt the thick, long, jet-black hair that he refused to cut, felt the wedge of muscle of a man it would be so easy to be immoral with, understood exactly why women lost their heads to him, for she was losing hers.

She moved her hand down to his shoulder, her fingers sliding to his neck, but Juan's hands halted hers and moved them onto his chest. It jolted her, just a little, for in that moment not a fraction of their bodies had seemed out of bounds. Cate had been utterly lost but she returned to common sense and he felt it, their eyes opening together, and she saw the regret in his as she pulled her mouth back.

'We could be so good together...' His forehead was resting on hers and she was struggling to get her breath.

Yes, they could be so good together but he would be so bad for her.

Cate wasn't looking for forever but neither was she looking for one night, or one week.

She simply couldn't do the casual thing, never had and never could. Could not walk into work tomorrow with everyone knowing she had succumbed to Juan's undeniable charm.

How she wanted to, though.

How she wanted to give in to the urges that were pulsing through her as much as the music coming from his home, how she wanted to just say, yes, I can handle this. Except, stupid her, her body came attached to a heart that was already a bit bruised and did not need to be shattered by him.

Oh, it would hurt to have him and then not. That much Cate knew.

'Get over him, Cate!' Juan said.

She was so over Paul, not that he knew it. Cate did not dare reveal the truth, so she made a wry joke.

'By getting under you?'

'No,' Juan said. 'I want you on top. I want to watch you come.'

He was bad.

He was dangerous.

He was everything she wanted and yet everything she didn't.

'Thanks for a lovely evening.'

'Would you like to go out tomorrow?' Juan offered.

'No, thanks.'

'Cate…'

So she took a breath and told him, 'I'm not what you're looking for.'

'You don't know what I'm looking for.'

'I don't know what I'm looking for either,' Cate admitted, 'but it's not…' she tried to think of the right word and she didn't know how best to say it '…you.'

'Ouch.'

Cate smiled and climbed into her car and caught the lingering fragrance of Juan from when he had been in her vehicle, the expensive note that overrode others.

She knew that she hadn't hurt him.

Ouch would be sitting in the staffroom in a couple of weeks' time, hearing who he'd slept with next, or, if they did last the little time he had left in Australia, ouch would be waving him off at the airport. Ouch would be having had him and then trying to move on.

Cate had just ended one serious relationship—a

rebound with the name Juan attached to it was heading way too far in the other direction.

She reversed out and waved to him, and, yes, she regretted it plenty. She could see them alone in his bedroom. Many times she had envisaged him kicking those boots to the floor and letting herself be a notch on his temporary bed; many times she had wanted to let loose and be as superficial and as laid back about things as Juan.

So clearly she could see it now, could still taste him on her mouth as she drove off, her bra around her waist, her cheeks burning, her hands willing her to turn round and return to him.

Instead, Cate chose safety.

CHAPTER FOUR

JUAN WOUND UP the party and did not invite anybody else to stay the night.

As the last taxi pulled off, he didn't even look at the clock or tidy up, he just undressed and headed to bed and tried to get Cate Nicholls out of his head.

She was way too serious for him.

Usually, he didn't want to hear about promotions and brothers and parts of the woman's history but with Cate somehow he did.

He thought about her hand on his neck, her fingers about to meet the thick scar and, no, he didn't want her knowing, would far prefer Cate thinking that he was shallow than to open up and confide in her...

That wasn't what this trip was about, he told himself as he lay there. Caught between awake and asleep, Juan was unsure if the kiss with Cate had been a dream, unsure even if his time in Australia was a mere figment of his imagination. He even wondered if Cate's words to Reece would disappear the second he awoke and he would find out it was all just another dream—because he was back there again, back in his head, trapped in his mind with a body that refused to obey even the simplest command.

In Juan's dreams he ran, his feet pounding the warm pavement as he dragged in the humid air.

In dreams, he threaded his beloved motorbike through lush Argentinian hills and made love to every single woman who had ever flirted with him—and there were many, perhaps Cate was one?

In his dreams, Juan jumped off bridges and felt the sting of icy-cold water as he plunged in.

In his dreams, he skied down mountains and did all the things he had never had time to do—Juan's focus had always been Martina, family and work.

He could hear the nurses, doing the two a.m. rounds, approaching the four-bedded ward, and Juan tried to haul himself out of the memory, tried to get back to kissing Cate, except he couldn't dictate his dreams and he couldn't erase his memories, and as the REM stage deepened a very natural reflex occurred.

'Hey, Juan.'

'I apologise.' Juan didn't need to look at the mirrors placed over his bed to know the sheet was tenting and that he was erect; instead, he stared at the ceiling as Graciela tried to catch his eye. 'Juan, it's natural,' Graciela said. They spoke in Spanish, Graciela, as always, practical—she was nearing retirement and had worked on the spinal unit for years. Graciela was more than used to young men finding themselves paralysed, used to the strange sight of a beautiful, fit body that might never move independently again and the humiliation a new spinal-cord injury patient faced regularly.

Yes, Graciela was kind and practical, it just didn't help now as she and Manuel rolled him onto his side. Juan was burning with shame in a bed in the Buenos Aires hospital he worked at.

Had once worked at.

Juan didn't want that part of his life over. Yes, he played upbeat for Martina and his family, insisted if there was a little improvement he could lecture and teach; but tonight the future, one where he could function independently, let alone hold another's life in his hands, seemed an impossibly long way off.

'Juan…' Manuel tried to engage with Juan. 'We still don't know the extent of your injury. You have spinal swelling and until…'

Juan closed his eyes. He didn't want hope tonight, he felt guilty that compared to his roommates there was a thin hope that his paralysis was not permanent; he just wanted to close his eyes and go back to his dreams but he knew he would not get back to sleep, knew that this would be another long night.

'You need a haircut,' Graciela commented as she washed his face. 'Do you want me to arrange one for you?'

'No.' Juan made a weak joke. He had been on his way to get his thick black hair trimmed when the accident had happened—it grew fast and he had it trimmed every couple of weeks. Always he had prided himself on looking immaculate, dressing in exquisitely cut suits and rich silk ties. Tonight those days seemed forever gone. 'I'm not risking that again.'

'How's Martina?' Graciela tried to engage Juan as they started the hourly exercise regime, moving his limbs and feet and hands. Martina had been here until eleven and Juan had pretended to be asleep the last two times the nursing staff had come around. It was important to know what was happening in the patients' lives as they adjusted to their injuries. 'Is she still worrying about moving the wedding date?'

There was a long stretch of silence before Juan finally answered, 'We broke up.'

'I'm sorry, Juan.' Graciela looked over at Manuel, who took over the conversation.

'What happened?' Manuel asked. He wasn't being nosey—the mental health of their patients was a priority, and he chatted as he moved Juan's index finger and thumb together and apart, over and over—as they did every hour—and then moved to rotating his wrist. Both simple exercises might mean in the future Juan could hold a cup, or do up a button, or hold a pen.

'We just...' Juan did not want to discuss it, still could not take it in, could not comprehend how every aspect of his life had now changed. 'It was mutual.'

'Okay.' Graciela checked his obs and shared another look with Manuel. 'I'll see you a bit later, Juan. Hopefully you'll be asleep next time I come around and I won't disturb you.'

Asleep or not, the exercises went on through the night.

Graciela moved on to the next bed, leaving Manuel to hopefully get Juan to open up a bit. Since his admission Juan had remained upbeat, insisted he was dealing with it, refusing to open up to anyone, and Graciela was worried about him, especially with the news of the break-up. Relationships often ended here; patients pushed loved ones away, or sometimes it was the other way around and the able-bodied partner simply could not cope with a world that had rapidly altered.

'Hey, Eduard.' She smiled down at the young man,

who gave her a small grimace back and moved his eyes towards Juan's bed. 'Is he okay?'

'He'll get there.'

For the first time Juan didn't think he would.

There was one thing more humiliating than a massive erection in full view of the nurses. It was starting to cry and not being able to excuse yourself, not being able to go to another room and close a door, to thump a wall, not even being able to wipe your own snot and tears.

'Let it out, Juan,' Manuel said as he covered Juan with a sheet and saw his patient's face screw up and tears fill Juan's grey eyes.

'I…' He didn't want to let it out, he had held it all in and he wanted to keep doing so. There was young Eduard in the next bed. He'd only been here for three days and Juan didn't want to scare him—Juan had been trying to cheer him up today.

He just couldn't hold it in any more.

The sob that came out was primal, from a place he had never been.

'Good man,' Manuel said.

Juan lay there sobbing as Manuel wiped his eyes and blew his nose. He was in hell and humiliated and scared and everything he'd tried not to be.

'Good man,' Manuel said, over and over.

He'd been a good man, Juan thought. He'd done everything right, everything had been in place—an amazing career, a loving fiancée. He *had* been a good man.

'No more…' Juan said, incoherent almost as he sobbed.

But there was more and tonight he let it out.

Graciela stood there and wiped Eduard's tears as

they glimpsed for the first time Juan's desolation and rage, and she swallowed a couple of tears of her own.

All Juan's roommates cried quietly along with him. Two had been there before, giving in to the grief and the fear in the still of the night, and Eduard soon would. There was no privacy in their worlds right now and all the men had heard the painful exchange between Juan and Martina.

All were with Juan as finally he gave in and wept.

No one was with him, though, when, eighteen months later, Juan woke up in a foreign country, feeling the desolation all over again.

CHAPTER FIVE

'How has your week been?'

Cate stopped for a brief chat with her neighbour as both women headed for work. Bridgette and her husband James were both in the police. It was nice being neighbours with fellow shift workers and, over the summer, Bridgette and Cate had spent several afternoons lying in one or the other's garden and putting the world to rights.

'It's been good.' Cate smiled as she lied. It had been a long week spent trying not to think about Juan and trying not to worry about work. 'Have you had your interview?' Bridgette asked.

'Not yet, but I'm stepping in as Acting Manager on Monday.'

'So you're off the weekend?'

'No, I'm working it, but if I do get the job I'll have every weekend off.'

'No more shift work!' Bridgette exclaimed, and Cate gave a smile and a nod, then they chatted a bit about the unrelenting weather but soon enough Bridgette asked how Cate was doing since the break-up and if she'd met anyone else.

'Not really.'

'What does that mean?' Bridgette asked. She was far too perceptive sometimes!

'There is someone I like,' Cate admitted. 'Or rather there was. He's from overseas and he's heading off to New Zealand soon so, really, there's no point.'

'No point in what?'

'Starting anything.'

'What are you talking about?' Bridgette gave her a very queer look. 'He sounds perfect for having a bit of fun with after Paul! You're not looking for forever, are you?'

'No, but…'

'Let you hair down and live a little while you're single.' Bridgette held up her hand and flashed her wedding ring. 'While you still can…' She winked. 'I'll come around over the weekend and we'll have a proper chat.'

'Do,' Cate said. 'I'd like that.'

Cate drove to work and tried to ignore the small bubble of disquiet that kept making itself known.

It had been the same towards the end of her relationship with Paul—everything had been going well, they'd got on, she'd cared about him; but when Paul had suggested moving in, they had been together for two years after all, Cate hadn't wanted that. When he'd suggested that they look for somewhere together, Cate had really had to sit and examine her feelings.

Cate turned on the radio instead—she didn't want to examine them now.

The staff car park was busy and Cate had to park well away from Emergency, which usually wouldn't matter but the temperature had barely dropped overnight and Cate couldn't wait to be in the air-conditioned hospital. The sky was a curious pink, even though the weather warned of no change or storms. Then, a week to the day after they'd shared that sizzling kiss, Cate saw him.

Only a madman would go running in this heat, Cate thought. An incredibly fit madman, though.

Juan was at the entrance to the hospital when she got there, trying to catch his breath before heading inside. He was bent over, his hands on his thighs, as he dragged in the sultry air. He was dressed in grey shorts and a top and they were drenched, as could be expected, given the considerable distance to the hospital from his apartment and that he'd run with a backpack on.

'Don't you listen to the warnings on the news?' Cate's voice was dry, deliberately refusing to reveal any awkwardness about their kiss last week. 'During a heat wave you're supposed to avoid exertion.'

'That is for the young and elderly,' he said, somewhat breathlessly bringing himself to stand upright, which was a bit disappointing for Cate as she'd been enjoying the opportunity of shamelessly looking at his legs. Long and muscular, pale-limbed with black hair and with a weight around one ankle. Briefly she wondered why, but only briefly—because as he looked down and spoke to her there was another image now to add to the Juan file she had stored away in her head. Juan smiled and added, 'And I am neither young nor elderly.'

'I think it was a given that no one would be crazy enough to go running in weather like this,' Cate said, trying not to blush, because now he was standing upright he looked amazing—he wasn't just unshaven, he practically had a beard. Harry wasn't going to be pleased, though Cate didn't mind in the least. He looked like a huge sexy god, Cate thought, and then corrected herself, because that was probably a wrong thing to think. He looked like a huge sexy…man.

It would just have to do.

'If a bit of heat and humidity stopped us, then no one in Argentina would ever run,' Juan said as they started walking into the hospital.

'So you're working here today?'

'They caved again.' Juan grinned. 'I got a call late last night to ask if I could come in for the morning shift.'

'You've been coming here for nearly three months now,' Cate pointed out. 'If you'd just signed the contract in the first place—'

'I've liked working all over Melbourne,' Juan interrupted, still slightly breathless. 'I've met loads of great people. It has been good not being confined.'

'Confined?' Cate frowned. 'It's not a prison.'

'Restricted,' Juan said. 'I don't know the word I am looking for in English,' he admitted.

'Doesn't it drive you crazy, though?' Cate asked. 'Never knowing where you'll be from day to day.'

'I love it,' Juan answered. 'It's the best thing I could have done.'

Cate could think of nothing worse and she told him so. 'I worked for an agency when I was a student. I loathed not knowing where I'd end up, where they'd send me, who I'd be working with…' She gave a small shrug. 'Maybe I'm boring like that.'

'You're never boring.' He turned and gave her a smile, just enough of a smile to let her know that he was thinking about the other night. 'Are you going to Christine's leaving do?'

Cate nodded. 'Are you?'

'She invited me.'

He headed into the changing rooms and Cate went to the staff kitchen and filled a glass with ice from the machine and then poured a cup of black tea with sugar over it and took her drink into the staffroom, where it was lovely and cool.

'Morning...' Cate smiled at two familiar faces—Charlotte and Adam were sitting dressed in their pyjamas and watching television. 'Have you two had breakfast?'

'No, we haven't eaten anything.' Charlotte was the louder of the two. 'Daddy said he'd get us something from the canteen before he took us to childcare.'

'Do you want me to get you something now?' Cate offered, and when they both nodded Cate went back to the kitchen and made them some cereal and juice.

'Christine's not doing the jump any more,' Kelly said as Cate came back in and served up breakfast for the twins, 'so there's a space if you've changed your mind.'

'Not a chance,' Cate said. Some of the staff had come up with the idea of a skydive to raise some much-needed funds to refurbish the interview rooms—but even if the funds were needed, even if it was for a good cause, Cate could think of nothing worse than jumping out of a plane, let alone paying for it. She much preferred to keep her feet on solid ground.

In came Juan, with that potent post-shower scent that had Cate's toes curling in her shoes. He was wearing scrubs, yet he still had on his signature boots and he was simply like no other.

'We've got hospital razors, Juan,' Kelly teased. 'I can get you a couple if you can't afford them.'

'Ah, but then you'd have to suture me after,' Juan said. 'They are lethal.' He looked at the twins, who had paused in their breakfasts and were staring up at this very large, very commanding man. 'Hello,' he said and then made Adam laugh. 'Are you the new consultants that are starting?'

'No,' Cate said, 'the interviews only started this week. These are Harry's twins, Charlotte and Adam.'

'Daddy got called in,' Charlotte said. 'For a sick boy.'

'Well, that's no good,' Juan said, and then looked at Cate's glass. 'Did you make me one?'

'No.' For a moment she thought he was going to take a sip of her drink.

For a moment he thought about it!

'Hey, Juan.' Kelly wasn't going to miss an opportunity for a little extra Juan time. 'A space has opened up on the charity dive next Sunday. You like all that sort of stuff.'

'I do.' He went and read the notice. 'I'll still be here. I fly out on the Tuesday…'

'We'll all go out afterwards,' Kelly said. 'It could be your leaving do.'

'Another one,' Cate said, and he turned at the slightly tart note to her voice but just smiled.

'Are you doing the jump?' Juan asked her.

'Absolutely not.'

'You should.'

'Why?' Cate challenged, but Juan gave no answer and went to get a pen from his pocket but, as usual, he didn't have one and he asked Cate if he could borrow hers.

'No,' Cate said. 'You already owe me three.'

'Just to put my name down on the list. I'll give it straight back.'

She ended up relenting and handed him her pen.

'Where are you going to next, Juan?' Sheldon asked.
'New Zealand! The south island first.'

'How long will you stay?'

'I'm not sure—I'll see how it goes, but I've heard that the skiing is spectacular, so I might stay there for the winter.'

'Then home to Argentina?' Sheldon asked as Juan wrote down his name to do the skydiving jump.

'I'm not sure...' Juan said. 'I was thinking of Asia.'

How could he have no idea where he was going? Cate wondered. He was hardly a teenager. He must be in his mid-thirties and just drifting through life, if you could call jumping off bridges and rafting down ravines and biking through the hills drifting. Cate just could not wrap her head around Juan's way of living.

'Come on, guys.' Cate glanced at the clock and stood. 'We'd better get round there.'

'You're not the boss yet,' Kelly teased.

No, she wasn't the boss yet, Cate thought. She said goodbye to Charlotte and Adam and turned on some cartoons instead of the news, telling them that someone would be around to check on them soon—but she wondered how she could tell Harry that he couldn't bring in the twins or, rather, if he did that the nurses wouldn't be watching out for them.

As they walked through the obs ward on their way, Cate was just about to ask the nurse who was working there to keep an eye out for Harry's children. But, seeing that the supervisor was there checking the bed status, Cate decided otherwise.

'Last day in the madhouse!' She smiled at Christine, who had just arrived at work.

Her smile wasn't returned.

'Thank God!' Christine rolled her eyes. 'If you can watch the floor, Cate, I'm going to go make sure all the ordering is up to date. Given all the fire warnings in place, I think it might be a good idea to order some extra burn packs and IV solutions...'

'I already have,' Cate said, and saw Christine's jaw tense.

'Of course you would have,' Christine said, and flounced off.

Cate knew she had annoyed Christine but, then, everything seemed to annoy Christine lately. Cate didn't particularly want to go to the leaving do tonight, especially now she knew that Juan would be there, but it would look rude and petty not to go. Handover was about to start and as she went to make her way over to the huddle Cate searched in her pocket for her pen, but of course, yet again, Juan had failed to give it back.

'Here...' He walked past and grinned as he saw Cate going through her pockets and he gave her back her pen, or what was left of it.

'You've chewed it!' Cate moaned.

'So did you,' Juan said, and opened his mouth and curled his tongue just a fraction. 'I had to taste you.'

He could be so filthy.

'Juan!' Harry came over to where they were standing, Cate's cheeks still on fire. 'I didn't know that you were on this morning.'

'Neither did I till late last night.'

'Well, it's really good to see you. Renée called me in a couple of hours ago—I've got a five-year-old named Jason that I'm really concerned about and am thinking of transferring. It would be great if you could come in and take a look.'

'Sure!' Juan said, and walked with Harry over to Resus as Cate went over to the group.

'Wow! I think Harry just gave Juan a compliment. He said that he was pleased that he was here. That's a bit of a turnaround.'

'I'm actually very glad to see Juan here this morning,' Renée, the night nurse, said. 'The child Harry is concerned about has got Goldenhar syndrome. Have you heard of it?'

Cate shook her head. There were many, many different syndromes, some relatively common, some rare, as was the case with this admission.

'It mainly presents as facial abnormalities. In Jason's case he's got a very underdeveloped left ear and he was born with a cleft palate and other problems. I've looked it up on the computer if you want to read about it. The main problem today is that he has presented with severe asthma, for which he's had several ICU admissions. Usually he's seen at the children's hospital and, understandably, the parents tend to stay close but, given the heat, they thought a couple of days near the beach might be nice.'

'It should have been nice,' Cate said. 'Poor things.'

'Yes, Jason has a very tricky airway and is really difficult to intubate—he's had to have a tracheostomy in the past. I think that was why Harry was so pleased to see Juan. The on-call anaesthetist has already been down to check on him a couple of times.'

'How come Harry is here?' Cate checked. 'I thought that Dr Vermont was on call last night.'

'He was,' Renée said. 'He was here till one o'clock but then he was unwell and had to go home. Jason came in just before five. I tried to get the paediatricians down but they're busy with a sick baby and so really I had no choice but to call Harry in.' Renée grimaced. 'I didn't realise that he'd have to wake up the twins.'

'Well, it sounds like Jason needed someone senior on hand,' Cate said. 'So, what else could you do?'

'Do you want to go in and take over?' Renée suggested. 'From Monday you'll be spending a lot of time in the office.'

'No, I shan't be.' Cate didn't elaborate, it wouldn't be fair on Christine, but Cate had no desire to disappear for hours into the office, as Christine all too often did. Still, Cate knew that she wouldn't be able to get as involved with individual patients—like it or not, the more senior she had become, the more hands off her role had been, so it was nice to take the opportunity to look after Jason.

Cate took the handover from Mary, the night nurse, as Juan examined the young patient.

'The parents are incredibly tense.' Mary pulled Cate aside. 'I don't blame them a bit, it must be awful to be away from all the specialists they need, but I think they're really making Jason more upset. Harry was talking about transferring him to the children's hospital and getting them to send out their emergency transfer team, but Lisa, the mum, got really distressed. Apparently Jason is petrified of flying, especially given that he's had more than his fair share of emergency transfers.'

They went through the drugs Jason had been given so far, before a grateful Mary headed for home.

Juan had been speaking with the parents, and had only just started to examine Jason. The little boy was exhausted but, despite that, his eyes were still anxious.

'So, you're a regular on the ICU at the children's hospital, are you?' Juan asked, after listening to his chest, and Jason nodded. 'I was working there last week and I'll probably be there again soon. Do you know Paddy?'

'We know Paddy,' Jason's mum said.

'Ken...do you know Ken?' the little boy said. He could still talk but only just.

'Do you mean Kent?' Juan checked. 'The ICU nurse?' Jason nodded. 'He's good fun. I might just have to give Paddy a call and let him know that you're here.'

Cate knew Juan was just putting the boy at ease, letting Jason know that he knew the staff there, while letting the parents know he worked there too.

He must be as popular there as he is here, Cate thought, strangely jealous of the other worlds of Juan.

'I just want a look in your mouth, Jason. Can you open it, please?' Juan removed the mask that was delivering medication and shone a light in. He looked carefully and then replaced the nebuliser, which was nearly finished.

'Okay, Jason,' Juan said. 'Just rest now and let the medicine start to work.' Juan looked over at Harry. 'Continuous nebulisers now...' Juan said, which moved Jason from severe to critical; but Juan seemed calm and Cate was a little surprised how Harry was stepping back and letting Juan take over the case. She knew Juan was good and a trained anaesthetist, but as it turned out Cate didn't know just how good he really was.

'He does need to be transferred, Lisa.' Juan spoke now to the mother. 'But I'm happy to keep a close eye on him here at this stage. I think we can wait for the rush hour to pass and then we will go by road ambulance...'

'What if something happens in the meantime?' Lisa was clearly petrified of being stuck in the outer suburbs without all the specialist doctors. But it was then that Cate realised exactly why Harry had been so pleased to see Juan this morning, and why he was so readily stepping back. 'What if something happens in the ambulance?' Lisa said, her eyes filling with nervous tears.

'I have worked with a lot of children who have similar problems to Jason,' Juan said, and went on to explain that he had spent a year as an anaesthetist in America, working at a major craniofacial hospital, and was very used to performing the most difficult of intubations on children.

'You've seen children with Jason's problems before?' Lisa asked.

'I have.' Juan smiled at Jason but Lisa still wasn't quite convinced.

'Jason had to be put on a ventilator the last time he had an asthma attack,' she said. 'They couldn't wean him off and in the end they couldn't keep the tube in his throat for any longer and so he had to have a tracheostomy...'

'Let's just focus on today,' Juan said, and started checking all the equipment. Harry had already brought over the difficult intubation box and Juan commenced pulling up drugs and taping the vials to the syringes, as relaxed as if he were making a coffee rather than preparing for a difficult intubation, and chatting away to Jason as he did so.

In a child with severe asthma everything was assessed clinically, there were no blood gases taken as it would simply upset Jason further. The fact that he was petrified of flying was an important issue because it was important not to distress Jason, but if he became much worse, there would be no choice.

'What's the protocol for IV aminophylline here?' Juan asked, after having another listen to Jason's chest.

'We don't give it here,' Cate said, because it was a drug that required constant monitoring. 'It's only given on ICU.'

'This has just become ICU,' Juan said. 'I'm not leaving him.'

Cate looked over at Harry.

'Fine.' Harry nodded and rolled his eyes. 'In Juan we trust.' Which actually made Lisa laugh.

'How long are you on till?' Lisa asked Juan.

'All day,' Juan said. 'Don't worry, when Jason is transferred I will go with him.' He didn't need to ask Harry's permission. Yes, it left them a doctor down, which would have to be sorted, but that was simply how it must be and no one argued. You could feel some of the tension leave not just Jason's parents but Jason himself. Clearly black boots and long black hair and an unshaven doctor didn't worry Jason a bit.

'Well,' Harry said, 'I'll leave you in Juan's capable hands and I'll come back in soon and see how Jason is doing.' He looked at Cate. 'I'm just going to get the twins some breakfast and then take them over to childcare.'

'I've already given them breakfast,' Cate said, and Harry gave a grateful nod. 'They're just watching cartoons in the staffroom.'

'Thanks so much for coming in, Doctor.' Jason's father stood and shook Harry's hand. 'It meant a lot.'

'Not a problem,' Harry said.

It was, though, a huge problem, and Juan commented on it after they had set up the aminophylline infusion and were waiting for the paramedics to transfer Jason.

Juan had double-checked that he had everything and Cate had done the same until, happy they were well equipped, they moved to have a quick coffee at the nurses' station, watching Jason from a slight distance. They had no idea when they might get another chance to take a quick break because they would both go on the transfer with Jason and then rush back to work at Bayside—unless there were any emergencies on the journey.

'Harry got here at five a.m. to see Jason,' Juan commented.

'I know.'

'Did he bring the twins in with him then?'

Cate gave a small worried nod.

'And does he do that sort of thing a lot?'

'Harry's wife died last year,' Cate said, by way of explanation.

'I know that,' Juan said. 'I asked if he did this sort of thing a lot.'

'He hasn't for a while.' Cate sighed because it was clearly starting all over again and on Monday she'd be the one dealing with it.

'He needs to get a nanny or someone he can count on.'

'He had a nanny,' Cate said. 'She just left.' She glanced at Juan, but he didn't return her look as he was watching Jason. But she did see him smile when she revealed a little more. 'They tend to fall in love with him.' She watched as Juan's smile spread further as he responded.

'Then he needs to stop sleeping with them.'

'Stop it!' Cate blushed, but trust Juan to get to the heart of it. Harry was a widower and a very good-looking, well-heeled one at that. There were plenty of women only too happy to bring over a casserole as Harry had once said with a wink and a tired roll of his eyes—he'd thought they were just being nice at first. No doubt he was having the same trouble with his babysitters. The thing was, it wasn't the Harry she knew. 'He adored Jill.'

'Of course he did,' Juan said. 'Sex and love are two very different things. I hear he was wild in his student days.'

'Please!' Cate said. She didn't even want to think about Harry and his sex life, but then she confided in Juan a little of what was troubling her. 'I've been told that once I'm Nurse Unit Manger I'm to address him bringing the twins in. Christine just ignores it, and Lillian says it's been going on for too long.'

'It needs to be addressed,' Juan said, and he glanced over just long enough to see the flare of worry in her eyes. That much he could do for her. 'I will speak with him about it.'

'And say what?'

'Bro talk,' Juan teased. 'You are not allowed to know.'

'But you barely know him.'

'Even better,' Juan said. 'Aside from everything, it's not fair on the little ones to be dragged in here all time.'

Had she thought about it, she would have expected him to take Harry's side, to say that it was no problem. Juan really was the most curious mix—the last thing she had expected was for him to actually be prepared to address the issue with the boss.

She'd love to be a fly on *that* wall!

CHAPTER SIX

JUAN DRAINED HIS mug and as they headed back, the paramedics arrived.

'So we're not competent enough for you, Juan?' Louise, half of the team that would be transferring Jason, teased as she walked into Resus with the stretcher.

'Jason has a very special airway, don't you, Jason?' Juan said.

Jason had, in fact, picked up considerably but he was on strong drugs that meant he needed very careful monitoring. All joking aside, it was good to have Matthew and Louise as the paramedics—they were an excellent team and Juan went through all the history and the equipment with them and told Louise the medications Jason was on.

'I want to get there quickly,' Juan said, 'with as little upset to him as possible.'

'Do you want one of his parents to come?' Louise checked, but Juan shook his head.

'I've already told them no. We're going to play chase.'

'Sorry?' Louise frowned but Juan just smiled.

There really wasn't room for either of Jason's parents to come in the ambulance, especially as there was the potential for an emergency on the way. Even with the anti-emetic he had been given, Juan was worried that Jason might vomit and that could prove urgent in itself with his poor breathing and difficult airway.

Fortunately, though, Jason was so taken with Juan and so delighted to have escaped the helicopter that he didn't protest in the least and neither did his parents. They headed off as soon as the paramedics arrived in the hope of beating the ambulance to the hospital. There was a good chance they might, as Juan took his time making sure everything was ready for the transfer, and ensured that Jason was as stable as he could be.

'Come on, then,' Juan said a good twenty minutes after Louise and Matthew had arrived. 'We've given your parents a good start, shall we see if we can catch them up? We might have to put the sirens on if we're going to have a chance.'

He winked to Louise, who smiled because she understood the game.

It was so much better with him than without, Cate thought as they sped with sirens and lights blazing to the city, trying to *beat* Jason's parents! The stars really had aligned for Jason today and they pulled up at the children's hospital without incident. Just knowing that Juan could deal with whatever presented had made a difficult transfer so much more straightforward. Juan was more than highly skilled—clearly his career had, at one time, been his major focus and yet here he was drifting around the world.

Cate wanted to know why.

She wanted to know more.

But soon he'd be gone.

'We got here first!' Juan said as the ambulance doors

opened and there was no sign of his parents. An exhausted Jason even managed a quick high five.

Jason was a direct admission to ICU and a very
pretty nurse looked up and turned purple before smiling when she saw Juan walking in. From the general
reaction to his entrance, Cate knew he was just as popular here as he was at Bayside.

'Juan!' A huge bear of a man came over and shook
Juan's hand. 'I thought you were in New Zealand by
now.'

'Soon! How are you, Paddy?' Juan said, and pro-
ceeded to hand over the young patient as, just a little
behind them, Jason's parents arrived.

'You beat us!' Lisa kissed her son. She was looking
a lot more relaxed in more familiar surroundings with
staff that she was more used to. 'How was the journey?'

'It went really well.' Cate smiled. 'Juan will come
and speak with you soon, he's just handing everything
over.'

'He's good, isn't he?' Lisa said to Cate, glancing over
to where Juan was chatting with Paddy.

'Very good,' Cate said, as Juan made his way over
to them.

'Okay, the journey was without incident,' Juan said
to Lisa. 'I've spoken with Paddy about all that has been
done for Jason and you are safely in the right place.'

'Thank you so much.'

'No problem,' Juan said. 'I am just glad he is here
without any more drama for you.'

'Well, we won't be going far again,' Lisa said, but
Juan shook his head.

'Did you have a good week?'

Lisa nodded.

'Would he have got the asthma anyway?'

Lisa was nearly in tears as she nodded again.

'So he is here, where he would have been anyway, but also he has had a week at the beach, and that is a *good* thing.'

He gave Lisa a cuddle, just a brief one, told her what an amazing mother she was, and Cate felt a sting of tears at the back of her eyes as Juan peeled another strip off her heart and nailed it to the Juan wall in her mind.

Don't go!

She stood there and looked at him, hating that very soon there would be no more Juan. She didn't even try to fathom her strong feelings towards a man she didn't really know, because everyone was crazy about him, everyone wanted more Juan in their life.

He shook Jason's father's hand and, oh, what the hell, Juan gave him a hug too and then went to say farewell to Jason. Cate was more confused than she had ever been, because she didn't want, ten days from now, to have Juan gone from her life and to have done not a single thing about it.

Then he spoiled it by going missing as they were about to head back to Bayside.

'I'll go and find him,' Cate offered.

She soon did!

Talking to Nurse Purple Face and making her laugh.

'You're quiet,' Juan said as they rode back in the back of the ambulance with Louise.

'I'm just tired,' Cate lied, not sure if she was jealous or just cross with herself. Or was it regret that she simply couldn't push aside her usual rules, wave her knickers over her head and give in to him?

'Well, that was worth the trip for me,' Juan said, 'I

have my shifts for next week all sorted I am working Friday through to Saturday on ICU there.'

Cate glanced up.

He only did one or two shifts a week, she knew that, preferably one long one, and he'd just been given that.

Today really could be the last time she saw him.

Apart from tonight.

CHAPTER SEVEN

CATE WAS SO distracted she didn't even hear Matthew talking on the radio until he called out to Cate and Juan. 'We've got an eighty-six-year-old in an independent living facility, she's waiting to be admitted for a chest infection but she's developed chest pain. Are you guys okay with us accepting?'

'Sure,' Juan said. 'So long as you go fast.'

On went the lights and sirens and Cate felt a flurry in her stomach as the ambulance sped off.

'You love this part, don't you?' Louise smiled.

'I do.'

'Are you still thinking about joining us?'

Cate shook her head. 'It's not for me. Sometimes I do still think about it, though.'

'You've thought of being a paramedic?' Juan's eyes widened in surprise.

'Cate came on a ride along with us,' Louise told him. 'About six months ago, wasn't it, Cate? I said to try a Saturday night in the city before she made up her mind.'

Cate could feel Juan's eyes on her.

'You didn't like it?' he asked.

'I loved it,' Cate said. 'It was an amazing experience but...' She gave a small shake of her head. 'It made me appreciate even more all the back-up that we have in Emergency, and I decided that it just wasn't for me.'

They were pulling into the independent living facility—the gate had been opened for them and a staff member directed them to the small unit where the patient was. Matthew and Louise took all the necessary equipment and then the four of them walked into a small house that was crammed full of furniture—huge old bookshelves and old-fashioned sofas—that looked a little out of place in the more modern surroundings.

'Her name's Elsie Delaney,' the on-call nurse explained. 'We had the doctor in to see Elsie last night for her cough and she was started on antibiotics for a chest infection. When I went to check on her this morning, she didn't look well and finally admitted she had chest pain. She's very independent and didn't want me to call you, of course.'

'Hi, Elsie!' Matthew walked in first and greeted the patient.

'What are all of you doing here?' came an irritated voice as the room started to fill up.

'You're getting the works today, Elsie,' Louise said. 'We had a doctor and nurse already with us, so that's why there are so many of us.'

The bedroom was as full of furniture as the rest of the house and, with Juan walking in front of Cate and his shoulders taking up most of the doorframe, it took a moment before Cate glimpsed Elsie.

She was tiny, sitting up in bed, her straggly white hair held back with a large, jewelled hair clip. She had a pink shawl around her shoulders and was wearing an elaborate necklace, and on her gnarled fingers were several rings.

She looked absolutely gorgeous, but she was wary and disgruntled and complained as Louise and Matthew did obs and attached her to a monitor while Juan slipped in an IV.

'I'm feeling much better,' she kept protesting.

Really, they weren't needed at all. Cate and Juan were completely supernumerary as Louise and Matthew had it all under control. They soon had a heart tracing and were giving Elsie some medication for pain and, despite having said she had little pain, as it took effect she lay back on the pillow. Elsie finally agreed that, yes, they could take her to hospital.

'Are there any family for us to inform?'

'She has a daughter, Maria, who lives nearby,' the nurse said, and spoke then to Elsie, 'I'll ring Maria and let her know what's happening.'

'She'll be very disappointed that I'm only sick and not dead,' Elsie said. 'It's the truth!' Elsie turned to Cate and winked, and Cate found herself smothering a smile. 'Does Maria even have to know that I'm going to hospital?' Elsie asked.

'Of course she does, Elsie!' the nurse answered. 'And you're wrong, Maria will be ever so worried.'

Elsie gave a huff to indicate that she doubted it. 'I'm not going out on a stretcher,' Elsie said.

'Fine.' Louise smiled. 'I'll go and get the chair.'

'Do you want to leave your jewellery here?' Cate suggested, knowing that one of the first things that would happen when they got to Emergency was that they would take it all off and lock it up in the safe. But Elsie wasn't going anywhere without her finery.

'And I want my photo album too…' She pointed to a shelf and Juan went over to fetch it.

'You might only be there a few hours,' the nurse pointed out.

'Then I'll have something to look at while I'm waiting,' Elsie retorted.

'Where's this, Elsie?' Juan asked, pointing to a picture in a frame where a younger Elsie was smiling into the camera against a stunning backdrop of houses and a glimpse of the ocean behind her.

'Menton,' Elsie said. The medication wasn't stopping her from talking! 'They call it the pearl of France. Have you been?'

'To France, yes,' Juan said. 'To Menton, no, but I want to now!' They chatted about it even as she was loaded into the ambulance and transferred from the chair to the stretcher. She was in a seated position for comfort and she and Juan chatted all the way to Bayside.

'I was there for six months,' Elsie said. 'Then I went back, oh, ten years ago now and it's still just as lovely.' She looked at Juan. 'Are you Spanish?'

'I'm from Argentina.'

'Well, I'll try not to hold it against you,' she said, and Juan laughed. Elsie peered at him for a while, slowly looking at his hair and then down to his boots before looking at Cate.

'He's a good-looking one, isn't he?' Elsie said.

'You just caught him at a good time,' Cate answered back.

'That's what I'm here for,' Juan responded, and Cate felt her cheeks burn a little, because a good time was *all* that he was here for—and she would do very well to remember that fact.

'So you don't live in Australia?' Elsie asked him.

'No,' Juan said. 'I am here for a working holiday.'

Elsie frowned for a while before speaking. 'You're a bit old for all that, aren't you?' And for the second time since meeting Elsie, Cate found herself suppressing a smile. Elsie was funny and wise and old enough to say what she liked and not care what others thought.

'Never too old, Elsie,' Juan said. 'Surely you know that?'

For the first time since their arrival it was Elsie smiling—at Juan. 'You're a charmer, aren't you?'

'Am I charming you, Elsie?' Juan smiled back.

Of course he was.

Christine didn't seem too impressed when they arrived back at the department. 'Finally, the wanderers return!' And she wasn't too pleased to have been forced out of her office during Cate's absence. 'I'm going to go and do some work now,' Christine said. 'There are incident forms to fill in. I don't want to leave them for you.'

'Sure,' Cate said, as Christine handed over the drug keys to her.

'She's a sour one!' Elsie muttered, as she was moved over onto a gurney.

Cate made no comment. 'I'm just going to go find you a gown,' she said to Elsie when she realised that there wasn't one. Now, that was one thing that *was* going to change when she was in charge. Cate really hated it when the cubicles were not properly tidied and stocked.

'Can't I just wear my nightdress?' Elsie grumbled, but Cate explained that she would need to take off her bra and necklace as the doctor would probably order a chest X-ray.

First, though, Cate did a routine set of obs and then headed off in search of the elusive gown. The linen trolley was void of them—the staff from the wards were always coming down and pinching linen from the emergency trolley and so Cate often hid a few pieces as soon as they were delivered. She went to her secret stash in the storeroom, where she kept a few gowns hidden behind the burn packs.

The phone was ringing as she made her way back and, with the ward clerk not around, Cate took the call—it was Maria, Elsie's daughter.

'She only just arrived in the department,' Cate explained. 'The doctor should be in with her soon.'

'She's talking?' Maria checked.

'Oh, yes!' Cate smiled, because Elsie hadn't stopped talking since she had laid eyes on her. 'Should I tell her that you're coming in?'

'No, no,' Maria said. 'I'll call back later this afternoon to see what's happening. It doesn't sound as if it is anything too serious. I don't know why they called an ambulance.'

'She developed chest pain,' Cate said. 'I'm quite sure it was more severe than even Elsie was letting on, though she's very comfortable now.'

'Still, I think an ambulance is taking things a bit far. We don't want any heroics.'

Cate blinked for a moment at the matter-of-fact way Maria addressed a rather sensitive issue. 'Is that something that has already been discussed?' Cate asked carefully. 'Does your mother have a DNR order?'

'No, but at her age surely we should just let nature take its course?'

Cate continued the difficult conversation, explaining that Elsie was lucid and comfortable and that it was something Elsie could discuss with the doctor if she saw fit. 'Is there any message that you'd like me to pass on to your mother?' Cate asked.

'Just tell her that I'll call back later,' Maria said, and then rang off.

Cate let out a breath, and when the phone rang again, on instinct she answered it, though she soon wished that she hadn't.

'Can I please speak with Dr Morales?'

'I'll see if he's available,' Cate said. 'May I ask who's calling?' As soon as the words were out she regretted them; she had made it clear that Juan was here but her mind had been so full of Elsie and her daughter that she had forgotten Juan's little lecture from last week.

'Tell him it is Martina.'

She found Juan in with Elsie, taking bloods.

'Sorry I took so long, Elsie,' Cate said. 'Your daughter just called...'

Elsie rolled her eyes and dismissed the information with a flick of her hand. 'You can ring her when I'm dead,' Elsie huffed. 'That will cheer her up.'

'She's going to call back later,' Cate said, making a mental note to speak to whichever doctor Elsie was referred to, so that Elsie's wishes could be discussed properly. 'Juan, you've got a call too—Martina is on the phone for you, I'm very sorry, I forgot and I—'

He interrupted her excuses. 'Tell her that I am with a patient,' Juan answered, labelling the vials of blood he had taken.

'Just to have her call back in ten minutes?' Cate checked, because Martina called fairly frequently. 'Why doesn't she ring your mobile?'

'Because I've blocked her.' He muttered something

under his breath in Spanish but then winked at Elsie. 'Excuse me, I need to take a phone call.'

'Be nice when you do,' Elsie warned, and Juan smiled and gave a small shake of his head.

'It gets you into more trouble sometimes.'

It did.

Juan had tried being nice, had tried being firm, had been downright rude a couple of times and the calls had stopped for a while. But as the date of what would have been their first wedding anniversary approached, Martina was more determined than ever to change history.

'Juan, I was hoping to speak to you.'

'I'm at work.'

'Then call me from home.'

'Martina—'

'You won't let me properly explain,' Martina interrupted. 'And I'm hearing from everyone the ridiculous things you are doing—that you are going to do a season of skiing. Why would you take such risks?'

'I'm not your concern, Martina. You made that very clear.'

'I would have come round. Juan, please, we need to speak.'

'Stop calling me at work,' Juan said, and hung up and sat for a moment, thinking of the man he had once been, compared with the man he was now.

Martina didn't know him at all.

She couldn't.

Not even *he* knew yet who the new Juan was.

'Poor Martina,' Elsie had said as Juan had left the cubicle to take the call and Cate had laughed. She loved old people, they knew about a thousand times more than the whole of the staff put together. It had taken

Elsie about two seconds to work out what a heartbreaker Juan was.

'I had one like that once,' Elsie said, nodding to the curtains Juan had just walked through, as Cate helped her undress and get into a gown.

'What, a six-foot-three Argentinian?' Cate quipped.

'No, a five-foot-eight Frenchman!' Cate wanted to put Elsie in her handbag and take her home. 'I was in my fifties and I'd been widowed for two years.'

'That's young to be a widow.'

'Don't waste any sympathy, I had a terrible marriage,' Elsie said. 'You can call me the merry widow if you must, but I was just sick of feeling like I was in my daughter's way and being told what to do. I took myself off to France—I'd always wanted to go and I was so glad I did. We had one week together and I had the best time of my whole life!' She pointed to a large silver bezel-set amethyst ring on her finger. 'No regrets from me,' Elsie said. 'We had completely different lives, it would never have worked long term but we kept in touch a little bit. He sent me a card now and then, and when he died ten years ago I went back and visited his grave and thanked him.'

She opened the album and showed Cate a picture of the love of her life, a love that had lasted just a few days.

'Have you ever been adored?' Elsie asked, and Cate frowned as she met Elsie's pale blue eyes.

'I don't think so,' Cate admitted, as the reason for her break-up was delivered to her, as the word she had needed was revealed.

'I highly recommend it,' Elsie said. 'Have you ever adored anyone?'

And Cate faltered. 'Adored?'

'It's a rare kind of love,' Elsie said, 'and I got to taste it.'

'Was it worth it, though, Elsie?' Cate asked. 'Lugging a broken heart around for the rest of your life.'

'My heart wasn't broken.' Elsie smiled. 'It soars every time I think of him.'

Cate's heart wasn't soaring, though, as Juan pulled her aside a while later and warned 'for the third time' that she had to have a word with the nursing staff and receptionist and remind them about privacy on the phone. They were not to reveal any of the staff rosters.

It was the closest she had come to seeing him angry or, rather, very disgruntled.

And so too was Cate, as she had a word with the staff as per Juan's instructions!

There she was, mopping up the chaos of his love life. It was a relief not to have slept with him.

Then she saw him laughing with Elsie, chatting with her as she was waiting to be moved to the ward, just standing by her gurney and putting a smile on the old lady's face. She was in a white hospital gown now, all the rings and jewellery off, but she had her pink shawl around her shoulders and was smiling as she showed him pictures.

No, it was no relief not to have slept with him.

It was simply self-preservation.

CHAPTER EIGHT

'CATE?'

Cate heard her name being called over her side gate as she hung out her uniform. She was in a rush, she'd just come out of the shower and, yet again, she was driving, so she really didn't have much time. But that never stopped Bridgette, who would chat happily as Cate got ready.

'Come over, Bridgette, but I can't chat for long.'

'Going out?'

Cate nodded. 'Yes, and I have no idea what to wear.'

They headed into the kitchen and Cate put on the kettle and did her usual thing with tea and ice—it was the only way to get through the long hot summer. Then they headed upstairs to decide what Cate should wear. 'I need a new wardrobe,' Cate sighed.

'So do I.'

'No, I really need one,' Cate said. 'Everything I've got I wore when I was going out with Paul. I've got my black dress, my going-out-for-dinner dress, the dress I wore when I met his family...' It was hard to explain.

'What about this?' Bridgette pointed out Cate's lilac skirt.

'It's the one new thing I have but I wore it last week.'

'Are you missing him?'

'No,' Cate said. 'And then I feel guilty that I don't.'

'So who's this other guy?'

Cate was about to shake her head but there was no chance of Bridgette meeting Juan and it would be so nice to get her advice—even if she had no intention of taking it! Bridgette was a lot more open-minded than Cate and always made her laugh.

'There's a casual doctor at work,' Cate said. 'He's from Argentina and is travelling for a year or two...'

'Nothing wrong with a younger man.'

'He's not younger, though,' Cate said, because, yes, most doctors were in their twenties when they travelled the world. 'He's in his mid-thirties, I think. It sounds like he had a really good job and then just took off...'

'He's a bit young to be having a mid-life crisis.'

'He's not in crisis!' Cate laughed. 'He's having a ball. He's stunning, everyone fancies him, he makes no bones that he's moving on soon and that he's not interested in anything serious, not that it stops anyone.' She paused for a moment. 'He works all over Melbourne and from what I saw today he's having just as much fun at the other hospitals as he is at Bayside, but...' Cate took a breath '...we get on, he likes me...'

'And you clearly like him.'

Cate nodded. 'He leaves the country soon so it's not going anywhere except bed...' She looked at Bridgette. 'And that's just not me.'

'Who knows where it could lead?'

'No.' Cate shook her head. 'That's the one thing I

can't let myself think. The whole point is, it *will* go no-where and I don't know if I can get my head around that.'

'You take things so seriously.'

'I know I do,' Cate said. 'I don't want to, but I do. I want to be carefree, I want to just let loose and have fun and live a little…'

'Then do.'

To Bridgette it was that simple.

Maybe, Cate thought, it could be.

She thought of Elsie and her one wild fling, thought of Juan, who was, quite simply, beautiful, and she felt as if she was standing on the edge of a diving board and peering down.

She wanted to have done it, wanted to be climbing out of the water, high from the thrill. It was just throwing herself over the edge that Cate was struggling to come to terms with.

'I've got a dress you can have,' Bridgette said. 'It's too big for me but it would look great on you. It's still got the tags on. Go and get ready and I'll fetch it.'

They borrowed and swapped things all the time. Bridgette was always buying and selling things on the internet. Cate did her make-up until Bridgette returned.

'Oh!' She stared at the dress. 'White?'

'First after Paul.' Bridgette winked. 'You need sexy undies.'

Cate opened her top drawer and let out a sigh. Juan was right, her relationship with Paul had gone on too long—two years in and they'd long since passed the sexy underwear stage.

'You are joking?' Bridgette said, as Cate pulled out

some rather plain white panties. 'You'd be better off not wearing any!'

Well, that wasn't going to happen—so she had to wear the sensible ones.

Cate never usually wore white, but when she put it on she found it suited her. The dress tied under the bust and scooped a little too low and certainly, when she looked in the mirror, the word virginal didn't spring to mind.

'It's too much! Or, rather, it's way too little,' she said, pulling the dress down over her bottom.

'Go for it,' Bridgette said. 'Take a taxi.'

'I'd rather drive,' Cate said. 'Anyway, I'm working tomorrow.'

She put on her new wedges and there was a flurry of nerves in her stomach as she looked in the mirror, and then there was the most terribly unfamiliar feeling as she filled her bag not just with lipstick and breath mints but with a few condoms too.

It was so not her.

Just so against her nature.

Cate picked up Kelly and Abby and kept having to force herself to keep up with the conversation, her mind was so full of Juan.

There was a flurry of hellos as they entered the garden to the restaurant where Christine's leaving do was being held.

They had chosen outside, not just because of the balmy heat but because thirty Emergency workers tended to be loud at the best of the times.

Cate slipped into a seat beside Louise and, although she did her best not to look over, the second she arrived she searched for him. She saw that Juan was already there. He was, of course, in the middle of the long table, sitting beside Christine and enthralling his adoring audience.

Maybe, Cate thought, all this indecision was for nothing, because he'd barely looked in her direction.

Maybe she'd said no one too many times.

'He could have his pick, couldn't he?' Louise said.

'Almost,' Cate sighed, they both knew who she was talking about.

'It's a shame he's leaving.'

'I just don't get the drifting-around-the-world thing,' Cate said. 'He wouldn't even commit to a three-month contract. I could understand it if he was in his twenties.'

'I don't need three months with him...' Louise nudged, and Cate pushed out a smile.

It was actually a very nice night—at first. The restaurant was set high on Olivers Hill and looked over Port Phillip Bay. The view was stunning and the drink was flowing a bit too freely because Christine's laughter was getting louder and louder, the stories at the table more outrageous. Cate laughed and joined in but her heart really wasn't in it. She just wanted to go home, not to be sitting waiting for a sliver of Juan's attention, not to be like Christine and hanging onto his every word.

And, yes, it hurt that he hadn't so much as spoken to her once.

It was still, at eleven p.m., unbearably warm and Cate blew up her fringe as she let out a long breath. 'Another sleepless night, tossing and turning...'

'Well, if you insist.' Juan's voice from behind her made Cate jump but she managed to answer in her usual dry fashion when she turned round. 'In your dreams, Juan!'

He lowered his head and gave her a brief kiss on the cheek, just as a few other colleagues had, but because it was Juan he took the tease one step further. 'Often.'

'You don't know when to stop, do you?' Cate really tried not to take his flirting seriously, for pity the woman who believed that any words that slipped from those velvet lips hadn't been used many times before.

'I brought you a drink…' Juan put a glass of champagne on the table.

'It's very nice of you, but I'm driving.'

'You can have one.'

'I don't want to have one.'

'I'll have it.' Louise smiled.

'Help yourself.'

He moved into an empty seat beside her—a few of the gathering had gone to dance and once she'd finished her drink Louise drifted off to join them.

'Are you looking forward to Monday?' Juan asked.

'I don't know that much will change,' Cate attempted.

'Of course it will.'

'It might only be temporary,' Cate pointed out. 'I might not get the job.'

'You know you will.' He saw the swallow in her throat. 'Is it what you want?'

'Of course it is.'

'Why?'

'Why wouldn't I?' She gave a small shake of her head. She wasn't about to discuss her career with a man who had turned his back on his.

'Have you thought about doing the sky jump?'

'The places are all taken.'

'You can have mine.' Juan grinned. 'I'd happily pay

to watch you jump out of a plane. I think it would be very freeing for you.'

'I don't need freeing.' Her eyes narrowed as she looked at him. 'I don't need a shot of adrenaline from jumping out of a plane to prove that I'm alive...' It annoyed her that he smiled. 'I don't.'

'I'm not arguing.' Still he smiled. 'I wish you good luck with your interview. If I come back in a couple of years, I expect you'll be carrying a clipboard and be the new director of nursing.'

'And what will you be doing in a couple of years?' Cate asked, because even though he was smiling she felt there was a challenge in his tone. 'Still roaming the globe, still doing casual shifts and not knowing where you're going to be each day?'

'I don't know,' he admitted. 'I try not to think that far ahead, but I am thinking ahead now—after you've dropped everyone off, come back to mine.'

'Pardon?'

'I would like to have some time to speak with you.'

'We're speaking now.'

'Okay, I would like to talk to you some more.' He would. Juan was more than aware that this might be the last time they were together and he cared enough about Cate to prolong the conversation. She clearly didn't want his career advice, so he switched track to something a little more palatable. 'I would like to be a bit more hot in my pursuit but I don't think you would appreciate it. You are senior, you don't need the Dr Juan walk of shame, so I'm inviting you to come over afterwards...'

'Why would I come back to yours?'

'Because, as I said when I brought your drink, I think about you often and think it is the same for you.

I believe if you want something you should at least try, and so I am.'

'I don't think—'

'Don't think, then.'

She couldn't really believe he could be so upfront about it.

'Juan...'

'I can't talk too long. Christine is being a pain and I don't want to upset her at her leaving do. We can talk some more back at mine.'

Cate excused herself and nipped out to the toilets. She wished for a guilty moment that she hadn't when she saw Christine in there in tears. Cate really didn't know what to say.

'It's hard, leaving,' Cate attempted, 'but you'll still keep in touch...'

'Do you really think I'm crying about that place?' Christine looked at her. 'I couldn't be happier to be getting away from it. It's Juan.'

'Oh.'

'I made a bit of a fool of myself,' Christine said. 'I asked if he wanted to come back after...' She cringed. 'I was very politely rebuffed. I told myself before I came out not to drink and Juan.' Cate gave a thin smile at Christine's pale joke—she knew exactly what she meant.

'Our livers will be thanking him,' Cate said, because she wasn't just being a martyr, driving everyone around—since she'd met Juan she'd been clutching water, terrified that a thimble of wine and all restraint would be gone.

'I should have known better.' Christine started the

repair job on her face. 'I knew it wasn't going anywhere, but it was so great being with him...'

Cate really didn't want to hear this; she didn't want to hear from Christine how good he was in bed. She was just about to excuse herself, skip to the loo, do anything to avoid that conversation. She had no idea what was coming next.

'It was all going great until you came back from leave.'

'What?'

'Oh, come on, Cate...'

'There's nothing going on between us.'

'I'm not blind.'

Cate just stood there; she knew this could get nasty and she certainly didn't have to explain one kiss to bloody Christine.

'What's going on between the two of you, then?' came Christine's slightly drunken demand.

'I don't know about you, Christine, but I left school years ago,' Cate said, and walked out.

She went to get her bag but she'd promised Kelly a lift.

Kelly could pay for a taxi for once, Cate decided. But there was no need to rush off. The drama was over—Juan had already gone.

Once the bill had been paid, even Kelly didn't want to head off to a club; so Cate drove her home and then dropped off Abby, which took her unbearably close to Juan's.

She couldn't just walk up the garden path for sex.

'Hi, Juan.' She could just picture it. 'I'm here.'

Cate was nothing like that, she did nothing like that. She had fewer regrets than Frank Sinatra.

Yet Cate didn't want to be sitting on a gurney in fifty years' time, speaking about this stunning six-foot-three Argentinian who had offered no strings, who had offered nothing but a night, maybe a couple of days...

'What did you do?' She could just see the young nurse asking her half a century from now.

'I went home.'

'Oh.'

'Nothing could have come of it,' Old Cate would rationalize. 'There was no point if it was going nowhere.'

Elsie would be disappointed

Bridgette too.

Even the imaginary nurse of the future would be disappointed in her tonight, Cate thought as she refused to give in to temptation.

She arrived home—there was a present on her doorstep and Cate opened the note with it as she stepped inside.

Hope you don't get this till morning and you can take this beauty out for a whirl tonight.
B xxx

Lilac velvet panties, still fresh in their pack, and they'd cost an absolute fortune, Cate knew, because Bridgette had been trying to sell them to her!

Wasted, she thought, crunching them into a ball in her fist and trying not to cry.

Lying in bed alone at two a.m., Cate was disappointed in herself too...at her wasted chance.

CHAPTER NINE

IN HIS NIGHTMARES he relived it.

Juan had waited for Cate until one and then given in and gone to bed, but he left the lights on outside and in the hall, just in case she changed her mind. He dozed off, trying to keep one ear open for her car, trying to fathom what it was about Cate that held his attention so, when he found himself back in his hospital bed.

'I felt that!' Juan said.

Manuel was washing his arm and Juan felt something, a vague sting, but at least he felt it.

His breathing came faster, scared to hope.

It was two a.m., the nurses were doing their rounds the night after his meltdown.

His roommates had all been wonderful.

'Love you, Juan,' André had called to him that morning as Juan had woken up. He was so ashamed for what he had put his roommates through, not knowing it was part of the process, not knowing two of them had done it too.

'Love you, Juan,' José had called, and Juan had closed his eyes.

'Does it make me gay if I say I love you?' young Eduard had called out, and Juan had smiled at the ceiling.

'No,' Juan finally answered. 'I love you guys, too,' he said. 'Thank you.'

It had been a day of conversation, a day of comradeship in the room as they'd stared up at the ceiling and joked and laughed. With the nurses' help they had even video-called each other that afternoon, finally face to face with each other. Eduard had told them about his amazing girlfriend, Felicia, who was currently flying back from a student exchange in France and would be coming in to see him tomorrow.

Juan had woken at two a.m., as he always did when the nurses approached.

'Not like this!' Juan's eyes snapped open as he heard Eduard shout. 'I don't want Felicia seeing me...'

Poor man.

Juan closed his eyes in agony as he heard Eduard screaming to Graciela, who was by his side. Poor man. Juan wept as Manuel wiped his tears and Eduard's deranged, grief-filled rant continued.

Oh, Eduard!

Juan wanted to go over and hold him. He wanted to fix him, to heal him, but all he could do was lie in respectful silence, grimacing over and over in agony as Eduard let out his fears in a room, in a ward, that understood.

Poor man.

Good man.

He looked up at Manuel, saw that his eyes were filling up too, but he gave a small smile of comfort to Juan.

'It's okay,' he said quietly. 'He will be okay.'

Juan's eyes snapped open and his heart was pounding as he came out of the memory. He moved his hands and it was luxury, checked that his legs still moved and then his hand moved to the heaven of an erection he could feel, even if was unsated, and he cried in the darkness, feeling the hell of that night again.

He sat up and gulped water and then reached for his laptop. He blew his nose as he made the call on his computer and waited for the comfort of a familiar face.

'Juan!' Eduard smiled as he came into focus.

'Does it make me gay if I call you in the middle of the night to tell you I love you?' Juan asked.

'Bad night?' Eduard asked, and Juan nodded as he wiped the tears from his face. Their friendship was worth more than gold, silver and platinum combined. It was Juan's most treasured possession. André struggled with Juan, jealous at his recovery, but they were trying to work through it. José was doing well and had movement in his arms and they kept in regular touch. But it was Eduard and Juan who were closest. The bond they had made back then was unbreakable and Juan smiled to see Eduard's cheeky grin. 'Bad luck for you if you are gay,' Eduard said. 'Felicia and I are getting married.'

'Eduard…' Juan was smiling and crying and then just smiling. Eduard was quadriplegic, with some small movement in his left hand and wrist. How he treasured that movement, how grateful he was for the exercises the nurses had performed over and over so that meant, with special equipment, he could type, could raise a beaker and drink from it. 'She is so beautiful,' Juan said. 'She is amazing…'

'I know.' Eduard was serious. 'Juan, will you be my best man?'

'We don't have best men in Argentina,' Juan teased lightly, but then he was serious. 'Except, for all that has happened, we do. I would be so proud to be your best man.'

'I don't want you to come home if you are not ready. I understand why you had to get away...'

'You tell me the date and I will be there. Nothing would keep me from being there to share in your day.'

'We are sorting the date out. Juan?' Eduard's tone changed to being tentative. 'There is something I wish to discuss with you. We're so grateful, but you don't have to keep paying for my pills.'

'Are the pills working?' Juan asked, and grinned as Eduard gave a shy smile back. This was no crude conversation, there was nothing they did not discuss, and Juan, loaded with survivor guilt, refused to leave anything out of bounds.

'Yes,' Eduard said. 'We have sex and it is getting better. She enjoys it, I think, and I love her pleasure.'

'Then that money is there,' Juan said. He knew the tablets were expensive and the young couple could not afford many, knew what must sometimes be on Eduard's mind, so he said, 'If I kill myself doing all this crazy stuff I have left money for you in my will. You will be pleasing your beautiful Felicia all your life, my friend.'

'Thank you.'

'No need,' Juan said, and he meant it.

'I tried what you said with my mouth,' Eduard said, 'and she was not faking!'

'I'll teach you more tricks another time,' Juan said. No, it was no crude conversation—younger, far less experienced, Eduard had cried and cried to Juan about losing his ability to make love to Felicia, had doubted that he might ever please her again. But even as Juan smiled, it faltered. His tears were coming again, and he felt guilty because he was the one walking and yet he was the one crying. 'Sorry, Eduard, you don't need this today...'

'Hey!' Eduard said. 'It's me.'

'I know.' Juan looked at his friend and nodded, because they had agreed it went both ways. For it to work, Eduard had to be there for him too. How different Juan was from how he had once been—how much his priorities had changed since that day.

'I was going to call you on Sunday,' Eduard said. 'I know it will be a difficult day.'

It would have been Juan's first wedding anniversary.

'It's not just the wedding anniversary,' Juan admitted. 'I like someone, Eduard. For the first time in what feels like for ever there is someone that I cannot get out of my mind and yet I cannot get her into bed.'

'You can.'

'I leave a week on Tuesday.'

'You have to leave?'

'Yes,' Juan said. 'My visa expires and anyway I don't want to get too involved.' He trusted so few now, had sworn never to let go of his heart—to just love them and leave them. 'She reminds me a bit of your Felicia, she is loyal, she is so serious...' He smiled as he spoke. 'She is so sensible and cautious but I am sure she is wild too...'

'You've got it bad,' Eduard said. 'Have you told her about the accident?'

'No.'

'Will you?'

Juan shook his head. 'No, I don't want her sympathy.' He shared it with no one apart from the people who already knew. 'I don't want to even try to explain what happened, what it was like.' Juan thought for a long moment and Eduard patiently sat through his silence. 'I don't want to get involved or anything. Really, I just want it to be a week on Tuesday and to be gone…I think.' Juan honestly didn't know how he felt. 'Perhaps it is just that she has said no. Perhaps that is the reason I can't forget her. If I could sleep with her, maybe I'd get her out of my mind.'

'Have you cooked for her?' Eduard said, and Juan grinned. 'Has she had the full Juan treatment?'

'No.'

'Go!' Eduard said. 'Sort it now.'

Juan laughed.

They chatted a little while longer then said goodbye and Juan found himself naked in the kitchen at three a.m. He lit the gas under the frying pan then he went and put a towel around his hips to save the precious bits from any oil splashes.

Hopefully he'd be needing them tomorrow night!

CHAPTER TEN

CATE WOKE TO the heat of summer and the scald of her own thoughts about Juan, insisting she should be proud of herself.

Imagine how much worse you'd be feeling if you'd slept with him, Cate tried to tell herself as she took her uniform off the line and quickly ironed it. *Imagine how much worse you would be feeling if you'd gone and got involved with him,* Cate told herself as she drove to work.

She had almost convinced herself she was proud for resisting, but it actually felt horrible, walking into the department and knowing she wouldn't see Juan.

That she probably wasn't ever going to see him again.

These last few weeks, when she should have been missing Paul, when she should have been trying to get over a two-year relationship, when she should have been sorting out what she wanted from her career, instead her thoughts and emotions had all been taken up with Juan.

Funny that a heart could be so raw and bruised by a man she barely knew when it was not damaged by the man she had spent two years with.

It surely just showed how right she had been to end things with Paul.

Cate looked at the roster, devoid of Juan's name, and thought of the sky jump next Sunday.

Her last chance to see him.

A farewell shag before he flew? Oh, God, she was actually thinking about it, Cate realised. *That* was how much she regretted saying no last night!

'How was Christine's leaving do?' Harry yawned. He had been working all night and was now about to go off duty until Monday.

'Good,' Cate said. 'Who looked after the twins last night?'

'Mum.' Harry sighed.

'Are you having any luck with getting a new nanny?'

'I've got a couple of people to see next week,' Harry said. 'But most of the people on the agency books want to live in the city, not a good hour away from it, and I've got the consultant interviews too.'

'Any luck?'

'Nope.' Harry shook his head. 'Same problem I'm having with the nannies—all the good ones want the bright lights of the city. Honestly, Cate, I need to sort something out as soon as I can. I can't keep just dropping everything and coming in because we don't have enough staff...' Harry shook his head. 'At least I don't have to think about it for a couple of days now. The department is Dr Vermont's problem this weekend. I'm going to spend some quality time with the twins.'

'You have a good one,' Cate said.

It was, thankfully, a busy morning, so there wasn't much time to dwell on Juan and the night that had never happened, but it was there in the back of her mind, just waiting for her thoughts to turn to it, and Cate was determined they would not.

She was heading off to lunch, having decided to spend the hour sorting out what would be her office come Monday. She did not want to sit in the staffroom and join in the post mortem about last night. There always was one after a department do. As the late staff trickled in, more and more would be revealed—who'd got off with who, who had said what, and people were already talking about Christine and the fool she'd made of herself last night.

Cate simply didn't want to hear it. She was just about to hand the keys to Kelly when she saw a well-dressed woman, looking a little lost, and Cate asked if she could help her.

'I've been told to come here to get my mother's valuables,' she said. 'I don't know who to ask for.'

'I can help you with that,' Cate said. 'Do you have the receipt?'

'Yes, it's in my bag.' She started to open it.

'It's okay,' Cate said, 'you can give it to me when you need to sign.'

Cate walked with her towards Reception, where the valuables safe was located. 'What ward is your mum on?' Cate asked, really just making polite conversation.

'She was on the emergency medical unit, but she passed away last night...'

'Oh.' Cate turned in surprise. She was used to upset relatives coming down to collect their loved one's valuables but this lady didn't seem upset in the least. Cate had assumed she was just collecting a relative's things to take home. 'I'm sorry to hear that,' Cate offered.

'It's a blessing really,' the lady said as she handed her the receipt and Cate looked down and saw Elsie's scrawling signature on the piece of paper. 'She just sat in her bed or her chair all the time, staring at photos. She couldn't really get out—it's no life!'

Cate didn't really understand the blessing. It might have been considered a blessing if Elsie had suffered a serious stroke or had been struggling with dementia, or had been in chronic pain. But, no, as she filled out the paperwork and Maria chatted on, it became apparent that Elsie had passed peacefully in her sleep—the nurse had gone to check on her at two a.m. and had found Elsie deceased.

Yes, perhaps it was a blessing to slip away like that, but as Cate handed over the envelope that contained the necklace and rings, tears were stinging at the back of her eyes. She wondered if the daughter had just sat down and spoken to her mother—if she had found out all the wonderful things her mother had done, all the stories Elsie had still been able to tell—would it have seemed such a blessing then?

Cate headed to the office and surprised herself when she started to cry, and it wasn't just over Juan, and that he was gone, her tears really were for Elsie. Death was commonplace here and so, of course, there were tears at times, although not usually for an elderly lady who had died of natural causes. Elsie had been so lovely and Cate had been so glad to know her even for a little while. She blew her nose into a tissue and when the phone rang in her new office, Cate picked it up with a sniff and gave her name.

'Are you crying because you regret not coming back to mine last night?' She heard his deep voice and smiled into the phone.

'Of course I am.' Cate attempted sarcasm, although she was speaking a bit of the truth.

'Or are you crying because you miss me?'

'It's just not the same here without you, Juan,' Cate teased, and then told him the real reason for her tears. 'Actually, I just found out that Elsie died in the night. I know she was old and everything...'

'She was a complete delight,' Juan said. 'She had a wild side to her, you know...'

'I heard about it!' Cate smiled. 'So, what can I do for you?'

'Well, this morning I went on a culinary trip of the Mornington Peninsula. We caught our own fish and then when we got back we cleaned and prepared them and were taught how to cook them...'

'That's very tame for you.'

'I can be tamed at times...' He said it in a way that had Cate blushing. 'So, I have some beautiful fish steaks that tonight I'm going to prepare with a *chimichurri* sauce, which I will serve with cucumber salad. I don't have a deep fat fryer so I cannot do *papas fritas*...'

'Sorry.' Cate frowned, not just because she didn't understand some of the words, more that she did not understand why he was reeling off a menu.

'French fries,' Juan translated.

'Haven't you heard of frozen chips?'

'I don't believe in them.' Juan tutted and Cate found herself both frowning and smiling at his strange response.

'So,' Juan said. 'Do we get to say goodbye, just the two of us? Will you join me tonight for dinner?'

Cate thought of Bridgette and the nurse of the future. She thought of Elsie and her Frenchman and then thought of a life with too many regrets, and even though she had been teasing him before, yes, Cate would miss Juan when he had gone.

It might as well be for a reason.

'Fish and salad sounds lovely.'

'Good.'

'What time do you want me to get there?'

'Whatever time suits you,' Juan said. 'I'll see you when I'm looking at you.'

Cate put down the phone. She couldn't wait until he was looking at her!

'No regrets, Elsie,' Cate said to the room.

She didn't feel quite so brave at six p.m.

What to wear when you knew it would be coming off?

Yes, she could eat her fish, have a lovely conversation and then go home—he wasn't going to be tying her to the bed, or maybe he was?

Strange that Cate shivered just at the thought, when she had never thought of such things before. But what she had meant was that Juan wasn't going to be forcing her.

She was consenting to be bad.

For the first time in her life.

Cate put on the lilac skirt and it would have to be the black halterneck again, though she loathed the strapless bra that squashed into her breasts and made her look like she had four. Then she remembered, with a thrill low in her belly, how easily he had removed it and the exploration of his hands during their one kiss.

Cate left it off.

Hardly daring, as she didn't have the biggest bust, but for sensible Cate it felt reckless.

And it felt even more reckless when she took off her skirt and shaved in a place she rarely did, her fingers lingering on her mound as she thought of Juan and what was to come.

'Me,' Cate said with a shocked giggle, and then dried herself and put the lilac velvet panties on.

She stopped for some wine on the way to Juan's, asking for help to choose one that went well with fish. She took the suggestion of a nice refreshing white but, as she approached his house, Cate worried about bringing wine—if she did, would he assume she was staying?

Was she staying?

Of course!

Cate had no idea what she was doing, even if Juan might think it easy for her. The thought of getting through the meal, knowing there was this big sexy slab of Argentinian for dessert, made her glow like the bush fires that were still raging.

When she got to the bottom of the hill, she was just about to turn the car round and go home, but the thought that he might see her doing that forced her to push on. She was determined not to appear nervous, absolutely determined to enjoy her one wild night, and, taking a deep breath as she approached his home, Cate parked and climbed out.

Juan opened the door before she knocked, took the wine and grinned, and she was relieved when he didn't welcome her with a kiss, for she was almost petrified of touching him.

'Did you go to the store on the corner of Beach Road?' Juan asked.

'Yes, why?'

'He suggested this one to me, too. I am still not up on

Australian wine.' Juan led her through. He was wearing black jeans and a silver-grey shirt and there was his bottle already open. He was chopping up cucumbers, it would seem, and sexy music was on.

'We put this one in the fridge...' Juan said, and took it. He went to get a glass, but first he seemed to remember what he had forgotten to do at the door. He gave her a brief kiss on the cheek, a sort of European greeting kiss, which was very nice and very friendly and very tame...

She glanced down to see that he was barefoot. Cate had never found feet sexy, but his were: he had very long toes, which made her aware that her own toes were curling. His eyes were looking not at her but at her oiled and scented body and at two thick nipples that were poking out like two mini-erections. There was a throb between her legs and, for safety's sake, she should have worn a bra, Cate thought.

'You're shorter without your high heels on.' Cate said and, as she spoke, even Cate didn't recognize her own voice—it was thick and loaded with lust—and it was then she found out how nice the wine she'd bought was, because she got a taste, and not from the glass.

He wedged her to the kitchen bench and she was kissing him back. Frantic, hungry, pre-dinner kisses. She wondered what on earth she'd been worrying about, wondered why on earth she hadn't spent the last few weeks being slammed up against his kitchen bench or taken on the floor.

'Sorry,' he breathed, prising his face from hers. 'That's why I didn't kiss you at the door...'

'It's okay.' Cate understood, she understood completely.

'I'll get you a drink,' he said, 'and then...'

Oh, what was the point? She was hauling him back now, because they *had* to have sex, they absolutely had to. Cate had never *had* to have sex before—it had never been an absolute command. Juan was kissing her again, lifting her up onto the kitchen bench and undoing the tie on her top.

'God, I've been wanting you for weeks,' Juan said.

She was naked from the waist up on the kitchen bench; she'd never been devoured like this before.

Not once.

Not once had she known the bliss of absolute un-bridled lust. His tongue was at her nipples, licking, nibbling, sucking. He uttered breathless words that he would get to them later, that now, just now... 'I have to be inside you.'

Cate's hands were just as busy as she almost ripped off his shirt, because she wanted to, *had* to, see the bits of him she hadn't seen before. She wanted to prove to herself, as if she needed to, just how delicious he was. Cate pulled his shirt down over his shoulders but it was difficult to get the last bit over his arms as he was face down and buried in her breasts, but the second his hands were free Juan was lifting up her skirt. It was as if she'd known him for ever, as if it was completely nor-mal to be heading for the zipper she was sliding down. Her only regret as she ran her hands over his delicious length was that, when she'd got ready for tonight, she had even bothered with panties.

Time really was of the essence but it didn't deter Juan; his fingers parted her and he was stroking her, his mouth a hot, wet demand on the senses in her neck.

'I want to see you,' Cate said, as she just about

pushed him off. She looked down at the sight of him huge and erect in her hands and moaned with want.

'We have to go to the bedroom,' Juan breathed. He went to lift her but she resisted, frantically patting the bench for her bag. Yes, she was taking a chance tonight, but not a chance like that—and the groan of relief from him as she pulled out some condoms was her delicious reward for being sensible.

'Good girl...' Juan said, grabbing the foil.

He had it on in an instant, and she should be ashamed of herself, Cate thought, except she wasn't.

She didn't even get to take off her panties. He merely pushed them aside and, huge and precise, he was inside.

'Oh...' He said something in Spanish, something that sounded crude, that matched their mood. He switched to English. 'I want to see you too,' Juan said. 'I *have* to see you.'

He took the knife he had been chopping the cucumbers with. She was trying not to come, trying to stay still as he cut off her knickers, and she felt the twitch of him inside her as he tried to hold back too, his eyes devouring her, freshly shaved and just for him.

They watched for a moment, just for two decadent thrusts, before her legs were tight around him and there was no need to look any more.

No, need for 'Is that nice?' she thought as he bucked inside her. No, 'Like that?' or 'Is that better?'

There was absolutely no need for Juan to question her enjoyment or pleasure, for Cate was sobbing it to the room. Her nails were digging in his back as he came deep inside her, as nearly three months of foreplay exploded inside Cate and she pulsed around him in turn.

'Dirty girl,' he said, as she swore for the first time.

'Beautiful girl,' he said, as he shot inside her again, as her deep pulses milked him dry. Then as she tried to get her breath back while resting her head on his shoulder, as she looked down at the chaos of their clothes, they started laughing.

Juan still inside her.

'I needed that bad.' Juan kissed her, kissed her and chased away the embarrassment that was starting to come.

'So did I.'

'Now,' he said, sliding out, remarkably practical as Cate sat there feeling dizzy, 'you sit over there on a stool and I can get you that drink, and then I can concentrate properly on making dinner.'

'Did you just say what I thought you said?'

Had they just had sex?

'Yes,' Juan said. 'You are a bad distraction in my kitchen.'

CHAPTER ELEVEN

JUAN KEPT A very neat kitchen. All evidence was removed—he even tied up her halterneck for her—and then he parked Cate on a bar stool and threw her expensive knickers in the bin. He handed a glass of wine to her.

'Better?' Juan said.

'Better.'

She couldn't believe it. Five minutes in his house and she'd had the best orgasm she had ever had. She felt a little stunned, a little breathless but enjoying the view. She was sipping her wine as if it was normal to watch him cook and see the scratches on his back that had come from her.

'Can I help?' Cate offered, because wasn't that what you were supposed to say?

'Relax,' was Juan's response.

It was bizarre that, for the first time around him, she could relax properly.

Juan picked up the knife that had sliced her panties and with a smile that was returned he carried on chopping the salad.

He could chop too.

Fast, tiny, thin slices.

'You've done that before.'

'I helped in the family business,' Juan said. 'After school and during medical school. My family have a…' he hesitated for a moment, perhaps choosing the right word '…café.' He moved and took the fish steaks out of the fridge and she heard the sizzle as they were added to the pan.

'They smell fantastic,' Cate said. 'What was the marinade?'

'Chimichurri,' Juan said. 'It is Argentinian. There are many variations but this is my mother's recipe that I make for you tonight.'

It was soon ready and they took the food outside to the table that had been laid. There was even a candle and, as she took the seat looking out to the ocean, Cate blinked a little when he put a plate in front of her. It looked amazing.

'You can cook too!'

'You haven't tasted it yet.'

'Ah, but it's all in the presentation.'

'No.' Juan smiled as he sat opposite her. 'It is no good to look beautiful and taste of nothing, or, worse, when you do bite into it, to find out it is off.'

'Well, it's a treat to have someone cook for me,' Cate said. 'It's beans on toast more often than not at mine.'

Cate loaded her fork. Of course she was going to say it was lovely, of course she would be polite, she meant what she had said, it was nice to be cooked for, but, more than that, it could taste like cardboard and the night would still be divine.

'Oh!' She forgot her manners completely, spoke with her mouth still full as she took her first taste. 'It's amazing.'

It was. The fish was mild and so fresh it might just

as well have jumped out of the ocean and landed on her plate, yet the marinade... Cate was not particularly into food unless it was called ice cream, but there was a riot happening on her tongue.

'It is very fresh...' Juan took a bite '...and my mother's *chimichurri* is the best.'

'I think I'm having another orgasm,' Cate said.

'Oh, you will later,' Juan said. 'And you won't think, you'll know.'

But there was only so much you could say about fish and, with sex out of the way, conversation turned a touch awkward at first. They knew little about each other, and it was supposed to be that way, Cate told herself, but she couldn't help asking about his homeland when he spoke briefly about it.

'Do you miss it?'

'No,' Juan admitted. 'I speak to my family a lot and to my friends, of course.'

'What made you decide to travel?'

'The woman who rings...' There was a tight swallow in Cate's throat as she found out a little about the man. 'Martina. We were engaged but it didn't work out. I think when any relationship ends you start to question things,' Juan said. 'Don't you?'

'I guess.' Cate took a swallow of her wine.

'Did you?' Juan pushed, when normally he didn't. Normally he didn't want to know more, but with Cate he did.

'A bit.' Cate gave a slightly nervous lick of her lips and put down her knife and fork. 'That really was delicious.' She tried to change the subject, but Juan pushed on.

'Really, my parents were never pushy with my education. They thought I would join them in the family business but I wanted to do medicine, so I spent a lot of time studying as well as working part time for them. I never really took some time to do other things I wanted.' He gave a small shrug. 'Now seemed like a good idea. I think it is good to step back. It is very easy to get caught up in the rat race…'

Cate shook her head. 'I don't see it as a rat race. I have no desire to step off.'

'None?'

Cate took a deep breath, felt the bubble of disquiet she regularly quashed rise to the surface. 'I'm not sure that I'm happy at work.' She looked at his grey unblinking eyes. 'I'm not unhappy, but sometimes…' Her voice trailed off and Juan filled the silence.

'Is that why you considered being a paramedic?'

Cate nodded. 'But it's not for me.'

'What is for you?'

'I'm working that out,' Cate admitted. 'Don't you miss anaesthesia?'

'No,' Juan admitted. 'I expected that I would and I admit I enjoyed looking after Jason the other day, but I don't miss it as much as I thought I might. I had a lot of ego,' Juan said, then halted, not wanting to go there. 'I like Emergency, that was where I started, then I did anaesthesia and was invited to a senior role. I enjoyed it, but being back in Emergency I realise how I enjoy that too.'

'And your fiancée?'

'Ex.'

'Who still calls regularly.'

Juan grinned. 'She misses me, can you blame her?'

'Did it end suddenly?' Cate knew she was teetering

outside the strange rules of a non-relationship—it was just that she wanted to know more about him.

'Yes.'

'Were you…?' Cate's voice trailed off.

'I can't answer a question if you don't ask it.'

'Were you cheating?'

'No,' Juan said. 'I took our engagement seriously. It was ended by mutual agreement—now it would seem that she has some regrets.'

Cate looked at him, looked at that full mouth, slightly taut now, saw a flicker of pain in his eyes. He wasn't over her, Cate knew it.

And Martina wasn't over him, Cate could guarantee that. Imagine having that heart and losing it?

'All I've learnt is that nothing lasts for ever,' Juan said. 'So enjoy what you have now, live in the moment…'

'Well, that's where we're different,' Cate said, hoping that he'd leave things there, but Juan did not. His hand reached across the table and took her tense one.

'Why so cautious?'

She looked up, looked at him, and he saw the tiny creases form beside her eyes.

'We're just talking,' Juan said lightly, but he wanted to know more.

'Having three brothers makes you so…' She attempted to sound dismissive but it was an impossible task. 'All my brothers were quite wild, but my middle brother decided to steal a car with his girlfriend when he was eighteen,' Cate said. 'I was nine. He nearly killed his girlfriend—I just remember the chaos, the hospital, the court cases, what it did to Mum and Dad… "Thank God for Cate," Mum and Dad always said. I never caused them a moment's worry, I guess it became who I thought I was…' She looked back up. 'Now I'm trying to find out who I am. So, yes…' She gave a tight smile. 'I guess the end of a relationship makes you examine things.'

She was trying not to examine things a little later as they headed to his bedroom and she saw that huge white bed. She was trying to live in the now—except she knew she would remember and miss him for ever.

He undressed her and she was more nervous than when she'd arrived at his door as he took off his boots, as he kicked them to the floor, because a night in his arms was simply not enough.

He pulled her to the bed.

'You're shaking?'

'I…' She didn't know what to say. In Juan's world the bedroom wasn't the place to tell him you had the terrifying feeling that you loved him. 'The air-conditioning,' Cate said, and she lay there as he went to turn it down, lay in his bed and replayed his words, told herself she could just enjoy what they had now.

As he climbed into bed and started to kiss her, at first her response was tentative. It was too late to be chaste, Cate told herself, and, yes, there was the heaven of his touch.

She felt the skin of his back beneath her fingers, felt the strength of his arms pulling her closer, and she was a mire of contrary feelings, because she wanted this and yet she was scared to give in. His tongue was as necessary as water to her mouth, his scent embedded in her head for ever and his touch almost more than her heart could handle. Her hands moved over his shoulder, to his neck and then her fingers paused, felt the ridge at the back of his neck. Then Juan's hands were there, moving hers away.

Again.

Her eyes opened to him and they stared for a moment, still kissing, but a part of him was out of bounds and he felt her withdraw, knew that tonight was about to end, and he didn't want it to, so Juan moved to save it.

Cate felt the shift in him. It was more than physical—he dragged her back to him, not with passion but with self; he just brought her back to him with his mouth.

He kissed down her neck and to her breasts and Juan lost himself for a moment, just lingered. He wanted her hot beneath him, he wanted them both sated, or he usually did, but tonight he let himself pause. He tasted her skin and licked and caressed with his mouth and then moved down.

She could feel the scratch of his unshaven jaw, such a contrast to the warm wetness of his mouth.

'I'll be sitting on ice tomorrow.'

It was her last feeble attempt at a joke, because she felt like crying from the bliss. His mouth, his touch, was slow but not measured. There was no blueprint—he followed her gasps and breaths, guided by them. It was more than sex. Her hands went to his head to halt him, scared to hand herself over, and then she felt his tongue's soft probe and heard the moans from him—and she gave in to being adored.

Juan hadn't done this in a long time; he hadn't been so enchanted ever. He buried his tongue in warm folds and she gave in to his intimate caress. Cate wanted him to stop, because she could feel herself building, in a way she never had. She wanted the trip of orgasm, a textbook pleasing, not the new feeling of delayed urgency he stoked.

'Stay still.' He wasn't subtle, he held her legs wider open and she looked down at him. Every stroke of his tongue was dictated by her response and when she sobbed he went in more firmly; when she arched, his mouth held her down. He tasted her, he ravished her.

He adored her.

Why, she was almost begging as his mouth took her more fervently. Why did he have to take all of her? Why did he have to show her how good things could be? She was coming and fighting it; she was loving it and scared of it, scared of loving him.

Juan held her in his mouth and he just about came himself as he felt her throb and finally still.

'Cate.' He said her name as he slid up her body. He did not allow her time to calm; he had taken her rapidly once and she sobbed now as he took her slowly. It was torture to be locked with him, to be consumed by him, to gather speed together with each building thrust.

Cate arched into him, her orgasm a race down her spine and along her thighs. The powerful thrusts of him had her dizzy, the feel of his final swell that beckoned his end was like a tattoo being etched in her mind. And then he collapsed on top of her; incoherent thoughts were voiced. It was a moment she would never forget.

'We could have had three months!' Breathless, Juan berated the time lost to them.

Breathless, Cate thanked God she had waited, because she couldn't have given him months of this with the end looming.

She was beyond confused; his bed was no place to

examine her true feelings, because she was only here for one night, except both knew they had just gone too far.

They both lay, pretending to be asleep, until finally they were—but it was an uneasy sleep, a difficult sleep. Cate didn't want to get too close to the man who lay beside her and Juan, with a mind that raced through the dark hours, chose not to hold onto her throughout the night.

Juan woke at two.

He always did.

He moved his legs, just a little, he moved his hands and then remembered Cate's hands on his neck and the look they had shared. He wondered if she might guess.

Asleep, she rolled into him and after a moment he put his arm around her; the luxury of that she could not know. He allowed himself the bliss of contact as he faced tomorrow—the anniversary of the wedding that hadn't happened was the day he had dreaded the most.

He dreaded another day now, one week on Tuesday when he left Australia. It was already drawing eerily close.

CHAPTER TWELVE

'*HOLA, MAMÁ!*'

Cate lay in bed, awaiting the promised coffee, but since Juan had got up his phone had rung three times and she had listened to him chatting away in the kitchen in Spanish, sounding incredibly upbeat.

Cate felt anything but.

Last night had been amazing, possibly the best night she had ever had, except she had got too close, had given away too much. Not just with words; last night had been way more intimate than she had intended.

Perhaps more intimate than Juan had intended too, for he didn't quite meet her eyes when he walked into the bedroom and waited while she sat up in bed and then handed her a mug. 'Sorry that the coffee took so long.'

'Is it your birthday?'

'No,' Juan answered. 'Why?'

'All the calls?'

'Just family.'

He wasn't so upbeat now; if anything, things between them were back to being a touch awkward.

'What time are you working?' Juan asked.

'Twelve,' Cate said, glancing at the clock. 'What about you?'

'I have the rest of the week off till Friday. I have to move out of here on Tuesday.'

'Where will you go?'

'I am staying with a couple of nurses I met, travelling, who work at the Children's Hospital.'

Nurse Purple Face, Cate thought. This was big-girl's-pants time: it was time to hide the truth and lie; it was time to smile and pretend it had been good while it lasted.

Good didn't even come close.

Cate gulped down her coffee and then climbed out of bed. 'Well, I'm going to head home.' She started to pull on her clothes.

'Have a shower,' Juan offered. 'I'll find a towel…'

'I'll get one at home.' She didn't want a beach towel or a Juan towel wrestled from a backpack. She wanted a cupboard with towels in it and a home that wasn't about to be abandoned without a backward glance a couple of days from now.

Even if the views were to die for.

Even if it had been fun.

'I'll see you.' He gave her a kiss and she returned it briefly, because it was very hard to not ask when, not to know if this was the last time.

'Cate…' He walked her to her car. 'I'll call you.'

'Sure.'

His phone was ringing again and she gave a cheery wave and drove off, her hands so tight around the steering-wheel that she turned the wipers on instead of the indicators as she turned into her street. She ignored the horn and the abuse from a driver behind.

She waved to Bridgette as she climbed out of her car.

'What time do you call this?' Bridgette joked, and

Cate gave another wave and bright smile but it died the moment the door closed.

Pull yourself together, Cate, she told herself.

She'd done it.

Slept with him.

Succumbed to him.

Now she just had to work out how to put together the pieces of her heart…

'Are you even listening?' Kelly asked as they sat in the staffroom, waiting for their shift to commence.

'Sorry?' Cate said. 'I was miles away.'

'It must be hell for those firefighters,' Kelly said, pointing to the news. 'Imagine having to wear all that gear in this heat and be near the fires.'

Cate couldn't imagine it. The fires were inching closer. It took up half the news at night and everyone was just holding their breath for a change to cooler weather to arrive, but there was still no sign of it.

They headed around to work and, though it would be tempting to hide in the office she still hadn't got around to sorting out, there were, of course, a whole heap of problems to be dealt with.

'I'm not happy to send him home, Cate,' Sheldon said.

There was a child, Timothy, who Sheldon had referred to the paediatricians. They had discharged the boy but Sheldon wasn't happy and wanted a second opinion.

Cate agreed with him, except Dr Vermont had called in sick.

Again.

Which meant there was no senior doctor to call in.

'What about Harry?' Sheldon said, but Cate shook her head.

'Harry needs this weekend,' Cate said. 'Unless there's a serious emergency, we should try not to call him. I've let him know that Dr Vermont is sick but...'

'What about Juan?' Sheldon suggested. 'He's senior.'

She could *not* face calling him, so instead she asked Frances on Reception to ring and ask if he could come in.

'He's not available today.' Frances came off the phone and then smiled as Jane, a new ward clerk, came over. 'I've got a job for you,' Frances said. 'Start from here and work your way down and see if you can get any of these doctors to cover from now until ten p.m. I've already tried the names that are ticked.'

Cate stood there as Timothy's screams filled the department and his anxious mum came racing out.

'Do you really think he should be going home?' she demanded.

'We're just waiting for someone to come and take another look at Timothy,' Cate said. 'Kelly, can you go and run another set of observations on him...' Cate let out a breath then turned to Sheldon. 'I'll ring Harry.'

Harry sighed into the phone when Cate called him and they briefly discussed Dr Vermont. 'He's never taken a day off until recently for as long as I've known him,' Harry said. 'Did he say what was wrong?'

'No,' Cate admitted. 'And I didn't really feel that it was my place to ask. I just said I hoped he got well soon and I would arrange cover.' She gave a wry laugh. 'Which is proving easier said than done on a Sunday afternoon. Sheldon is concerned about a two-year-old who's really not right. They've diagnosed an irritable hip and the paediatricians have discharged him...'

'Do you want me to come and have a look at him?'

'I want you to finally have a weekend off, without being called in.'

'Well, that's not going to happen for a while.' Harry let out another long sigh. 'Have you tried Juan?'

It was a compliment indeed that Harry was thinking of asking Juan to cover for the rest of the weekend because, despite his impressive qualifications, Juan only covered as a locum resident.

'We tried,' Cate said. 'He can't.'

'Okay, I'll be there in ten minutes but I'll have to bring in the children.'

'That's fine,' Cate said. 'I've got Tanya sitting in the obs ward, watching one elderly patient, I'm sure she won't mind.'

Juan ended the call with Frances.

He had thought for a moment about accepting the shift at Bayside but he knew that he might not be the best company today.

Martina would be ringing him soon, pleading with him to give them another go. She would say that she had just panicked, that in time, of course, she would have come around to his injuries.

Juan turned off his phone, not trusting Martina not to use a different number just so that he wouldn't recognise it and pick up.

He would go for a drive, Juan decided. For the most part, while in Australia, he had enjoyed not driving, but now and then he hired a car. It was just so that he could explore, but today he wanted to do something different.

Juan hired a motorbike—it was his main mode of transport back home.

Or once had been.

Juan felt the machine between his legs and guided it up the hills, felt the warm breeze whipping his face and arms, and he relished it.

The view was amazing; to the left was the bay, and ahead he could see the smoke plumes far in the distance where bush fires were still raging, swallowing hectares of land but thankfully no homes.

He had enjoyed travelling around Australia—it was an amazing and diverse country and it had been everything he needed. It had been the last few weeks that had made him feel unsettled, wondering if it was time to think of returning home.

He swallowed down a mouthful of sparkling water, thought about New Zealand and Asia, and was suddenly weary at the thought of new adventure. He just couldn't get excited at the prospect of starting over again, and finally he knew he had to acknowledge the day.

His family had been ringing all morning, trying to see how he was coping, whether or not he was feeling okay.

Juan really didn't know how he was feeling.

He sat there, staring into the distance, trying to picture how his life might have been had the accident not happened. He and Martina would have been married for a year now—perhaps there would have been a baby on the way by now.

Juan asked himself if he would have been happy.

Yes.

Then he asked himself if he was happy now.

There was no neat answer.

Juan dragged his hands through his hair and his fingers moved to the back of his neck. For a moment he felt the thick scar and recalled pulling Cate's hand away from it.

He hated anyone knowing.

Not just about the accident but about what had happened afterwards.

Still, eighteen months on, he could not quite get his head around the moment when everything had fallen apart—and it hadn't been the moment of impact.

Juan closed his eyes, remembered when he had looked up into the eyes of the woman he was due, in six months' time, to marry. He had realised then that it was not a limitless love.

Juan didn't want to dwell on it, he hated the pensiveness that swirled like a murky haze, that billowed in his gut like the plumes of smoke in the distance.

He should be enjoying himself, Juan told himself, heading back to his bike. He should be getting on with life, living as he had promised to on those dark, lonely nights when his future had been so uncertain. He should not be thinking about some imagined past that had never happened, a marriage that hadn't taken place. He should be embracing the future, living for this very minute, not dwelling on a wedding that had been cancelled and a future that had never existed.

He was happy being free, Juan told himself, and he intended to remain that way. He climbed back on his bike and started the engine, ready to move on with his life—as he had said to Cate last night, nothing lasted for ever. It was about enjoying what you had now—and Juan was determined to do that.

He *was* happy.

Juan rode the bike up the hill, along the curved roads, hugging the bends and telling himself he loved the freedom, loved the thought of a world that was waiting for him to explore it.

A small animal burst out of the bushes and his mind told him not to swerve, but instinct won.

The bike skidded and he tried to right it but failed. But he was skilled on a motorcycle and he was not going fast, so he controlled the landing. He felt the bitumen burn along his shoulder as he and the bike skidded into the bush, regretting that he had ridden without leathers.

Great.

He lay there a moment, getting his breath back, winded, a bit sore. His ego was a touch bruised, especially when Juan heard a voice and the sound of someone running towards him.

'Stay still!' He heard the urgent command. 'It's very important that you stay still.'

'I'm fine,' Juan called back, and moved to sit up, to get the bike off that was pinning him down.

'You *have* to stay still.' A man was looking down at him. 'I'm a first-aider.'

Brilliant.

'My wife's calling an ambulance.'

Better still!

'I'm fine, really,' Juan said through gritted teeth. 'If you could just help me move the bike.'

'Just lie still.'

'I know what I'm saying—I'm an anaesthetist,' Juan said. 'I work in Emergency…'

'They say that doctors make the worst patients.' Still he smiled down. 'I'm Ken.'

Trust his luck to get an over-eager Boy Scout come

across him. Juan lay there as Ken's wife came over, telling them that the ambulance was on the way.

'Hold his head, darling,' Ken said. 'I'll lift the bike.'

'What about the helmet?' She looked down at Juan. 'I'm Olive, by the way.'

'Don't try and remove it,' Ken warned. 'Leave that for the paramedics.'

His day could not get any better, Juan thought, lying there. Of course he could shrug them off, get up and stand, but they were just trying to help. He *should* be grateful, Juan told himself. Technically they were doing everything right, except, apart from a grazed shoulder, there was not a thing wrong with him.

He *was* grateful.

Juan looked up at Olive and remembered the last time he'd had an accident. He had been lying on his side, begging bystanders not to touch him, not to roll him, not to move him.

It's *not* like last time.

Over and over he told that to himself and held onto the scream that was building.

He'd explain things to the paramedics, Juan decided, closing his eyes and hearing the faint wail of a siren far in the distance. He tried to calm himself, but there was an unease building as he thought of the paramedics' response when he told them about his previous injuries. An appalling thought occurred when he tried to work out his location and the nearest hospital.

He did not want Cate to know.

Juan did not want his past impinging on the little time they'd had, yet he could hear the paramedics making their way over to him and knew that it was about to.

'Juan!' Louise smiled down at him, shone a torch in his eyes as she spoke to him. 'What happened to you?'

He told her. 'It was a simple accident. I have only grazed my shoulder. I'm not going to hospital.'

'Let's just take a look at you, Juan.' Louise was calm. 'Were you knocked out?'

'No.'

'How did you land?'

'On my shoulder.'

Her hands were feeling around his neck. 'Do you have any pain in your neck?'

'None.' He felt her fingers still on the scar and then gently explore it.

'Is there any past history that we need to know about, Juan?'

He stared up at the sky at the tops of the trees and he absolutely did not want to reveal anything, except only a fool would lie now.

'I had a spinal injury.'

'Okay.' Louise waited for more information.

'Eighteen months ago.'

He just stared up at the trees as the routine accident suddenly turned serious. 'I'm fine, Louise.' He went to sit up but hands were holding his head.

'Just stay still, Juan.'

'My neck is stable, better than before…'

'What injury did you have?'

'I had an incomplete fracture to C5 and C6.'

He lay there as they carefully removed the helmet and he was placed in a hard collar, and the spinal board was brought from the ambulance.

'I don't want to go to Bayside,' Juan said as they lifted him in.

'I'm sorry, Juan. We need to take you to the nearest Emergency.'

'Nothing is wrong.'

'We have to take all precautions. You know that.' Louise cared only for the health of her patients and pulled out the words that were needed. 'I'm following protocol.'

He couldn't argue with that.

The best that he could hope for was that Cate might be on her break, that he could somehow slip in and out of the department unnoticed by her. She might even be holed up in her office.

Except she wasn't Christine.

She wasn't like anyone.

Cate was like no one he had ever met.

Juan stared up at the ceiling of another ambulance and said it over and over again to himself.

It's not like last time.

CHAPTER THIRTEEN

CATE REGRETTED THAT she'd had to ask Harry, she truly
did, but she had never been more grateful about how
approachable Harry was than when he came in to examine young Timothy.

The boy was, in fairness to the paediatricians, mark-
edly more distressed by the time Harry arrived. Harry
took some bloods, called the lab and asked for the tests
to be put through urgently. Then he called the ortho-
paedic surgeons as it began to look more and more as
though the child might have septic arthritis, which was
a surgical emergency and needed to be dealt with as
quickly as possible.

'They're going to take him up for aspiration of the
hip under sedation,' Harry explained to Cate a short
while later, 'and they're getting started immediately on
antibiotics.' He was just writing up his admission notes
when Lillian, the director of nursing, came and asked
Cate if she could have a word.

'Over here.'

Lillian gestured to a place away from the nurses' station and as they walked up to the drug fridge and out of
Harry's earshot, Cate took a deep breath, because she
knew what was coming next. 'Why,' Lillian asked, 'is

the student nurse sitting in the observation ward, drawing pictures with Harry's children?'

'Because Dr Vermont, who was supposed to be the on-call consultant this weekend, has rung in sick. Sheldon was worried about a patient the paediatricians have discharged and luckily for us Harry came in. As it turns out, it would seem that the child has septic arthritis.'

'Then why,' Lillian persisted, 'is a student nurse, who should be getting clinical experience, acting as a childminder, instead of being out on the floor?'

'Because she was already rostered on the observation ward…' Cate was saved from having to explain herself further when she looked up and saw that Louise was signalling her to come over so that she could have a word.

'Excuse me,' Cate said. 'I'm needed.'

'We'll discuss this later.' Lillian said. 'This really can't continue.'

Cate knew it wasn't over yet, but for now she was happy to escape a lecture and walked over to Louise.

'What you got for us?' Cate asked.

'A very reluctant patient,' Louise said.

'So, what's new?'

'It's Juan,' Louise said, and Cate felt the colour drain from her face. 'He didn't want to come here but I've stuck to protocol and brought him to the closest Emergency. He seems okay…' Louise frowned at Cate's pale lips. 'He came off a motorcycle. He's got a few cuts and a nasty abrasion to his shoulder, but he's had a previous spinal injury.' Cate stood for a moment as she heard that it wasn't whiplash they were talking about, that, in fact, Juan had broken his neck and had been paralysed for a period. She could almost hear her brain clicking as things fell into place.

'Incomplete C5 and C6...' Louise said, and Cate remembered her hands being removed from his neck.

'There's a slight weakness in his left leg,' Louise continued, 'but he insists that since the accident there always has been.'

Cate recalled noticing the weight on his leg as he'd run and thought she might be sick. She really knew nothing about him, yet he had insisted on finding out about her.

'We've taken all precautions,' Louise continued. 'I said I'd come in and try to do this as discreetly as possible.'

'Okay.' Cate nodded. 'Bring him in.'

If she had thought it might be hard facing Juan after last night, it was going to be close to impossible now.

'It had to be you.' Juan gave a tight smile as she came over. He was staring up at the ceiling and only glanced at her briefly. There were a few scratches on his face and his shirt was torn and she could see that his teeth were gritted and that he was struggling.

'Well, they came and got the most senior nurse on.' Cate tried for practical, tried to hold onto a strange anger that was building inside her. She was about to add that if he'd asked to be dealt with by someone he hadn't slept with then he'd be lying on that stretcher for quite a while.

She tried to hold onto the shout that was building.

'I don't need to be here,' Juan said.

'Then you shan't be for long,' came her pale-lipped response.

They slid him over on a board and Cate held onto

the top of his head and then covered him with a sheet to undress him, but as she went to unbutton his shirt he asked that she not.

'I'll just do some obs, then.' Cate said, knowing how embarrassed she'd be if the roles were reversed. Not that she'd have been riding a motorbike through the hills with a previously broken neck.

Neither would she have been white-water rafting.

Or considering hitting the ski season in New Zealand or, next Sunday, diving out of a plane.

Her hands were actually shaking as she did his routine obs and then a set of neurological.

Juan answered her questions. Yes, he knew where he was and what day it was.

As if he could ever forget.

Yes, he could squeeze both of her hands tightly.

'Just get the doctor in to see me,' Juan said as she lifted the sheet to see two black boots.

'Lift your leg against my hand.' He did with the right.

'And the left.'

There was perhaps a slight weakness. Cate wasn't sure she would even have noticed had Louise not pointed it out.

'That leg has some residual weakness from my previous accident,' Juan said.

'I'll just take your boots off.'

'Please, don't.'

'It's fine.' Harry swept in and picked up on the tension. 'Juan, how are you?'

'I've been worse,' came Juan's wry response.

'So I hear.'

'I thought Dr Vermont was on this weekend,' Juan said to Harry.

'So did I, but I'm afraid you're just going to have to make do with me.' Harry was brisk and efficient as he started his examination. 'Okay, Juan, you know the drill.'

He went through today's accident with him, which Juan could remember clearly. 'A small animal came out of the bushes, I swerved...'

'And your past medical history?'

'Can we just...?' Juan closed his eyes in impatience. Cate thought he was about to ask for the collar to come off, or to say that it was all unnecessary again; instead she raised her eyes slightly at what he said next. 'Can you leave, please, Cate?'

Two spots of colour burnt on her cheeks as Harry turned round and smiled. 'We'll manage, Cate.'

Had it been a door and not a curtain, Cate might have slammed it as she walked out. She simply didn't know why—she was not upset, she was angry.

Harry went round with him for the CT and Cate tried not to let his dismissal of her sting.

She tried her best to not give a sarcastic response when Harry came to speak with her some time later. 'All the tests look good and Juan's neck's fine. I've had the orthopods take a look at the images. He's got a lot of titanium in there! He needs a dressing to his shoulder—'

'I'll get someone to do it.'

'Cate...' Harry sighed. They had worked together for a long time and he knew her well, though he hadn't guessed until now that there was anything going on between them—Juan was for too depraved for Cate, or so Harry had thought! 'Juan didn't ask you to leave because he didn't want you looking after him.' He shook his head and tried to explain. 'He's a proud guy,

Cate. He's been through a lot...' Harry let out a breath through his teeth. 'I told Juan that you'd be in to do his shoulder and he's fine with that. I want him in the obs ward for a few hours, he's a little bit tender over his left kidney but it all looks fine. I want his urine tested and to be sure he's okay before I discharge him, because there's no one at home. Hourly obs, and I'll come in this evening again to see him.'

'Thanks Harry.' Cate attempted to snap back to normal. 'I really am sorry to rot up your weekend.'

'It's not a problem,' Harry said. 'It just makes me more determined that we hire the right staff. This place is running on empty...'

Harry headed off with the twins and Cate buzzed Tanya to tell her that they would have a new admission in the observation ward soon; then she prepared a trolley to sort out Juan's shoulder. She could feel tears pricking at the back of her eyes as she set up but she swallowed them down before making her way in.

Someone, perhaps Harry, had helped him into a gown and his clothes and boots lay in a heap beneath the trolley next to his crash helmet. His cervical collar had been taken off.

'Harry wants your shoulder cleaned and dressed and I need to look at the scratches on your face. Would you like someone else to come in and do that?' Cate checked.

'Why would I want someone else?' Juan asked, although Cate could tell he was just as tense with the situation as she was.

'I just thought you might.'

'Just do what you have to.'

Cate sorted out his face first, cleaning a few superficial abrasions and cuts and closing them up with couple of paper strips. They didn't speak much; Juan was more than used to staring up at a hospital ceiling in silence.

'I need you to roll on your side,' Cate said when she had finished sorting out his face.

'For what?'

'So that I can pick the road out of your shoulder.'

The gown was far too small for him and hadn't been tied up at the back. The abrasion was large and it would take a while to clean it up. Cate moved his hair out of the way and could clearly see the thick scar that ran the length of his neck and the clips scars either side—the reason why he had always halted her hands.

'This might sting a bit,' Cate said as she squirted a generous amount of local anaesthetic onto Juan's shoulder. She knew it must sting but he didn't wince. While she waited for it to take effect, Cate took a moment to get some more equipment for her trolley so that she wouldn't need to keep going in and out—they both wanted this over and done with.

Silence dragged on as Cate cleaned his shoulder. Thankfully he was on his side, facing away from her. It was already hard enough without looking at each other—it was going to take a long time to do it properly, and Cate would have loved to take the opportunity to hide in an office.

She knew the severity of his previous injury and she could not believe that someone who'd been given another chance at life could take it so lightly.

It was Juan who broke the silence. 'Cate, could I just explain—?'

'The same as you, Juan,' Cate said through tight lips, 'I really don't want to talk about it.'

'Cate, the reason I didn't mention it is that I don't want to be reminded every five minutes about it. I don't like talking about it.'

'That's fine.'

'Am I supposed to have given you a full medical history before I asked you to dinner?'

Cate was saved from answering when Kelly came in behind the curtain. 'We've got someone on the phone enquiring after you, Juan.'

'We've been through this,' Juan said. 'Just say that you're not sure if I'm on duty and take a message.'

'The call actually got put through to Reception.' Kelly grimaced, not that Juan could see it. 'Jane's new, she's the receptionist on duty and she didn't realise that you worked here. She thought it was your girlfriend enquiring as to how you were after the accident. It's Martina…'

'What did she say to her?' There was an ominous note to Juan's voice.

'That you were in X-Ray and she told her to call back in half an hour or so. She has just—'

The expletive that came from Juan's lips was in Spanish and possibly merited.

'She's a bit upset,' Kelly elaborated. 'I've tried to reassure her but she isn't listening to me, so I brought the phone down. I thought if you perhaps could speak to her, she would realise that you really are okay.' Kelly handed him the phone and, still on his side, Juan took it.

'I'll leave you to speak to her in private,' Cate said, as it was already more than awkward. 'I'll come and finish doing your shoulder afterwards.'

Cate turned to go but as she reached the curtain Juan

called out to her. 'Cate, would you mind speaking with her, please.'

'Juan…' She could not stand to speak Martina, given she had been in Juan's bed last night—except that wasn't relevant here. Juan was a patient.

'She is my ex-fiancée,' Juan said. 'Someone I specifically asked your staff not to give any information to.' And then he lost the warning note from his voice. 'Cate, I really don't need this today, of all days.'

'Sure.' Cate took the phone, doing her best to simply treat him as a patient. 'What would you like me to say to her?'

'Just say as little as possible. Tell her that it was a minor accident and that I'm fine.'

Cate took the phone and introduced herself.

'I would like to speak with Juan Morales.'

'I'm afraid that's not possible. Can I help you with anything?'

'I want to know what is happening. I'm in Argentina. Have you any idea how stressful this is to not be able to speak with him?'

'Juan had a small accident this afternoon. He's got some abrasions, which are being dressed at the moment. Apart from that, he's fine and will be going home later today.'

'How did it happen?'

'I'm sorry,' Cate answered. 'I can't give out that sort of information without Juan's permission.'

'He does this!' She could hear Martina's mounting exasperation. 'He wants to pretend he has not had an accident. He's going to kill himself one of these days; he just pushes everyone who loves him away. I don't know what he is trying to prove. Today would have been our first wedding anniversary and instead he's lying in hospital…'

'Give me the phone.' She didn't know if Juan had heard what Martina had said but she handed him the phone and Juan spoke in short, terse sentences, before ringing off.

The silence was deafening as Cate resumed cleaning his shoulder.

'She seems to think that because we were once engaged—'

'Juan.' Cate was struggling to keep her voice even, could scarcely believe the information she had just heard, understood now why his family had all been ringing him. 'You don't owe me any explanation. I don't blame Martina for being concerned. If I cared about you, I'd be concerned too.'

'Ouch,' Juan said as her tweezers picked out a particularly deeply imbedded stone, and Cate even managed a wry smile—she had no idea if he was referring to her words or the sudden pain in his shoulder.

She had no idea about Juan at all.

But wasn't that the whole point of a one-night stand or a brief fling? It was why she simply wasn't any good at them.

She carried on pulling out some of the deepest stones. He tensed a few times but said nothing and Cate got on with her work, trying not to look at the scratches on his back.

The ones that were courtesy of her.

Kelly noticed them, though.

She came in to get the phone and to ask Cate to cast her eyes over an IV flask—a simple procedure, but be-

cause the solution contained potassium it needed to be
checked by two nurses. Cate nodded that all was fine.

'Your poor back, Juan,' Kelly said, eyeing the
scratches and giving Cate a wink as she walked out.

'It shouldn't be too much longer,' Cate said. 'And
then we'll get you round to the observation ward.'

'I don't need to be observed.'

'Harry thinks you do. If you choose not to follow instructions I'll get the necessary paperwork...'

'I'm not stupid enough to discharge myself.' He
turned, just a little but enough to nearly send the sterile
paper sheet flying. 'Cate, I didn't tell you because I don't
need your sympathy.'

'Oh, believe me, there's no sympathy coming from
behind you, Juan.'

'You're upset.'

'No. I'm not upset.'

'I can hear your voice shaking.'

'I am so not upset, Juan.' She shook her head. This
wasn't the place but, what the hell, she told him her
truth. 'I'm angry.'

'Angry?' This time he turned enough to knock off
the sheet completely and looked into her eyes and, yes,
she was angry all right. 'Angry, about what?

'It doesn't matter. I'm going to get Kelly to come in
and finish off your shoulder.'

'Why?'

'Because you're a patient and it doesn't look good
for a nurse to be shouting.'

'Don't worry about that—I'm fine with the conversation.'

'Well, I've got work to do.'

'I don't understand what you're angry about.'

'Your carelessness,' Cate answered. 'Your lack of limits...'

'You know what, Cate?' Juan was surly and in no mood to sweeten things. It had been one hell of a day after all. 'I don't think you're actually angry at me. I think you're more cross at your own...' He couldn't think of the word he wanted so hers would have to do. 'Limits.'

'I'm going to get Kelly.'

'Fine,' Juan said. 'Go and count your stock.'

It was lucky for Juan she had already put the tweezers down!

She asked Kelly to come in and take over and then walked to what would soon be her office. She took a long, calming breath and tried to remember what she'd been doing before she'd been called away for the problems with Dr Vermont.

Stock orders.

Cate drew in a less than cleansing breath.

And there were outstanding complaints and incident reports to be dealt with too. Despite promising to complete them, Christine had left them unfinished.

Damn you, Juan, Cate thought.

At least she knew where she was going; at least she knew what was happening from week to week—at least she wasn't ricocheting around the world with a handful of titanium in her neck.

She *was* hiding in her office, though.

But at seven p.m., when Tanya hadn't had her break, Cate had to go in and relieve her. Thankfully, Juan was asleep.

'His observations are all stable,' Tanya said. 'Harry

just stopped by and is happy for him to be discharged in an hour or so. Or, if Juan prefers, he can stay overnight.'

'I'm sure he won't want to.'

Tanya also told her about the elderly lady. 'She's waiting for a bed on the geriatric unit and one might be coming up soon. I've just done observations and they're all fine. She's very deaf and she refuses to wear her hearing aid but she knows exactly where she is and what is happening.'

'Thanks.' Cate smiled. 'Go and have a break and I'll keep an eye on them both.'

Cate was glad that Juan was asleep as she took a seat and saw that his obs had only just been done. Determinedly, she didn't read his notes. She didn't want to know about his past and she really wasn't in the mood for conversation. The director of nursing was, though.

'Where's Harry?' Lillian asked as she walked through the observation ward.

'He's at home.'

'He's still on call, though?'

'Yes.'

'Cate, something has to be done,' Lillian said. 'What if he gets called in tonight?'

'I believe he's making arrangements, although the consultants' childcare plans are not a nursing concern.' Cate did her best to terminate the conversation but Lillian was having none of it.

'It becomes a nursing concern when it's the nurses who end up watching the said consultant's children. Cate, you're the acting nurse unit manager.'

'As of tomorrow.'

Juan's eyes snapped open as he heard Cate's tart response. He hadn't been asleep for a moment, but since his time on the spinal unit he was exceptionally good at pretending that he was.

'Well, as of tomorrow, Cate, it will be up to you to ensure it doesn't happen.'

'That what doesn't happen, Lillian? That we don't ask Harry to come in when we're without a consultant or concerned about a patient? Is that what you want?' Cate looked her boss in the eye. 'I happen to be very grateful that the nursing staff have a consultant who, despite personal problems, is prepared to come in at short notice when he's not even rostered on. I'm very grateful to have a consultant who will accept a worried phone call from a member of the nursing staff and get in his car and come straight in.'

'It can't continue.'

'I'm sure Harry is more than aware that the situation is far from ideal.'

Juan lay there and listened as the director of nursing pointed out some health and safety issues. He listened as the nurse who had admitted she liked working in Emergency because of the back-up she received from her colleagues backed up a member of her own team one hundred per cent.

'What if one of the nurses can't get a babysitter?' Lillian challenged. 'We can't run a crèche in the staffroom!'

'I'll cross that bridge when I come to it.'

'Not good enough, Cate.'

'No, it's not,' Cate responded. 'And it's a poor comparison. If a nurse can't come in I can ring the hospital bank to have them cover a shift or I can ask for a nurse to be sent from the wards. We have ten nurses on duty at any one time, but there aren't very many emergency consultants to call on at short notice.'

He heard the director of nursing walk off and he heard a few choice words being muttered under Cate's breath and he couldn't help but smile, but it faded as Cate took a phone call and then came over.

'Are you awake?'

Juan turned over and looked at her. 'I am now.'

'How are you feeling?'

He gave a wry laugh.

'I just took a phone call from a Ken Davidson,' Cate told him. 'Apparently he helped you today. He said he waited until your bike was picked up.'

'Did you get his number?' Juan asked, relieved that the call hadn't been from Martina. 'I need to thank him.'

'I did,' Cate said. 'He's also got your wallet.'

'Thanks.' Juan said. 'And I'm sorry for what I said before about you getting back to your stock. You do a great job—I guess I was just spreading the misery.'

Cate gave a small nod of acceptance. 'Harry's happy for you to go when you're ready or you can stay the night.'

'I'll go home, thanks.'

'Do you want a lift when I finish?'

'Do you always offer patients a lift home?' Juan asked.

'I would offer any colleague a lift home in the circumstances.'

'Then that'd be great.'

It was either that or ask to borrow fifty dollars for a taxi.

For Juan, it was Indignity City today.

Juan borrowed a pair of scrubs and she watched him try not to wince as he bent down to pull on his boots.

He carried a bag containing his clothes and crash helmet and they walked, pretty much in silence, to her car.

It wasn't how it was supposed to have been, Juan thought. He loathed all his secrets being out, but now they were and, as he had expected, she was acting differently with him.

'Watch the speed bumps,' Juan said as she drove him home slowly. 'I might jolt my neck and suddenly have no feeling from the chest down.'

'You don't need to be sarcastic.'

'You're driving as if you have a Ming vase rolling around on the back seat,' he pointed out.

'I'm a careful driver,' Cate said, about to add, *unlike some of us*, but Juan turned and saw Cate press her lips firmly closed.

'I should have just run it over,' Juan said. 'I should have killed the baby koala bear.'

'It wasn't a koala,' Cate said, and she almost smiled. *Almost*. But Juan knew she thought he shouldn't have been out motorcycling in the first place.

'So, I am supposed to walk slowly, not run, not climb, not surf or ski...' He looked over at her. 'Athletes go back and compete after the injury I sustained. I am not doing anything my doctor does not know about. I walk everywhere, I run most days. I take my health seriously.'

'I get it.' Cate gripped the wheel.

'I don't think you do.'

'I get it, okay?' There were tears in her eyes as she realised he was right, and yet her fear had been real. 'I just got a fright when I heard how seriously injured you had been.'

He looked at her tense profile.

'Fair enough,' Juan conceded. 'Do you know how my

accident happened?' Cate said nothing. 'I was going to get a haircut…' He gave a wry laugh as Cate drove on. 'It was embarrassing really on the spinal unit. There were guys who had been diving, playing sport, car accidents—I had been walking to get a haircut. A car driven by an elderly woman mounted the kerb and really only clipped me, but the way I fell…' He let out a long, exasperated sigh. 'It was bad luck, chance, whatever you want to call it.'

'So now you take risks?'

'Yes, because I never did before and look where it got me, lying on my back paralysed from the neck down. Now I live, now I do as I please…'

'It's all just a game to you, isn't it?'

'It's no game,' Juan said. 'I have ridden a bike for years, it is how I get around back home. I'm not on some daredevil mission. I'm living my life, that's all.'

'Well, your fiancée is beside herself.'

'Ex.'

'Because you're too bloody proud and have too much to prove.'

'You don't know me.' His grey eyes flashed back; it was the closest Juan had come to a row in a very long time. It was the closest he had come to anyone in a long time and that was what he had been trying to avoid, Juan reminded himself as they pulled up at his apartment and he climbed out.

'I know that today would have been your first wedding anniversary,' Cate called to his departing back, and watched as he turned slowly.

'It would have been, except Martina decided she didn't want to marry a man in a wheelchair.'

Cate sat there, her knuckles white as she clutched

the wheel. Of all the things he might have told her, that was the last she had been expecting.

'Juan!'

She went to step out of the car.

'Please, don't.' Juan put his hand up. 'Thank you for the lift.'

'Juan,' Cate said. 'I didn't know.'

'Because I didn't want you to know.'

'I don't want to just leave you—'

'Why?' His eyes flashed. 'I want to be on my own. I don't want a heart to heart, I don't want to sit and talk, I don't want company.'

Cate bit her lip as he threw out his final line.

'I never wanted you to know. I never wanted any more than what we had.'

She watched his departing back and, yes, she should leave it there, except she couldn't. If Juan didn't want kid gloves because of his injury, or because of the phantom anniversary, then he wouldn't get them from her, she decided as she opened the car window.

'Why didn't you just leave it at sex, then?' She watched his back stiffen but he didn't turn round. 'It was supposed to be sex and dinner, Juan, but, oh, no, you had to delve deeper. You had to take it that step further and ask about me and my past and future. So much for living in the now!'

She didn't wait for his response. She knew she wasn't going to get one; instead, she drove off as Juan let himself into his home.

His temporary home.

What had they had? Cate asked herself.

A whirlwind romance?

Holiday fling?

A rebound after Paul?

Not one of them fitted.

They didn't fit for Juan either. He turned on his phone and saw the many missed calls. He looked around the empty apartment and told himself it was time to move on. The day he had dreaded was almost over, yet, instead of dwelling on the woman he should have married a year ago today, it was Cate who consumed his thoughts.

She was right—it had been more.

CHAPTER FOURTEEN

CATE HAD MORE than enough to keep her occupied.

Or she should have had.

Yet, despite working as Acting Nurse Unit Manager, despite telling herself over and over that Juan was not her concern, she could not stop thinking about him.

Through the week she attended meeting upon meeting, caught up with the backlog Christine had left and sorted out her new office. She was determined to make a stand and, even though there were so many other things that she should be doing, she put in mandatory appearances on the floor, though sometimes she wished that she hadn't. It felt different without Juan—even the knowledge that he might possibly be called into work, that she might see him again, had meant more than Cate had, until now, understood.

That was why she didn't do one-night stands, Cate told herself as she walked back from yet another meeting.

Then she felt her heart squeeze when she glimpsed him entering the department.

He had to save the best until last.

He was wearing black jeans and his boots but the silver buckle on his belt was larger than usual and the white, low-necked T-shirt he was wearing was too tight and showed his magnificent physique along with a generous flash of chest hair as well as his nipples. He hadn't shaved since she'd last seen him. He looked like a bandit, or an outlawed cowboy, Cate thought, waiting until he went into the department and then walking along behind him, almost willing him not to turn round.

'Juan!' Of course he was pounced on and Cate walked on quickly, rather hoping he had not seen her—his final words to her were still ringing in her ears and she wasn't quite sure she could pull off a farewell without tears invading.

Cate headed to her office and as she closed the door she let out a sigh. She'd left it neat but already her inbox was full again and there was a list of messages to attend to. Gritting her teeth, she went to take off her jacket but was interrupted by a knock on the door—she knew it was him.

'Nice jacket,' Juan said.

Cate loathed it.

She was to wear it to meetings, she'd been told, and it was an authoritative touch, apparently, if she was called on to attend to upset patients or relatives.

'How's it going?'

'I'll tell you when I find out.' Cate gave a terse smile. 'So far all I seem to do is sit in meetings.'

'Is that where you've just been?'

Cate nodded. 'I've just been to the nurse unit managers' meeting and after lunch it's the acute nurse unit managers' meeting!' She rolled her eyes. 'I didn't know that you were working.'

'I'm not,' Juan said. 'I had to come in and sort out the health insurance forms from my accident. It was easier to do it in person.'

There was a knock at the door, which was already half-open, and Harry popped his head in. 'Cate, I was just wondering if you could...' Harry's voice trailed off. 'Juan, I didn't know that you were on.'

'I'm not,' Juan said. 'I wanted to come in and say goodbye and I also wanted to apologise if I was a bit difficult on Sunday. I do appreciate all the care that was taken.'

'We do tend to panic a little bit when it comes to spinal injuries.'

'With reason,' Juan said. 'I was very lucky to recover so well—I know that is often not the case. I was also hoping to have a word with you before I go.'

'Of course,' Harry said. 'But you'll have to make it quick, I've got an interview in fifteen minutes.' He looked at Cate. 'I'm interviewing right through till six. If I run over, is there any chance that you could pick up the twins and watch them for five minutes?'

'I finish at five, Harry,' Cate said, and Juan watched her cheeks glow red as she attempted to say no to Harry and then gave in. 'Though I doubt I'll get away on time...' Cate gave a small flustered nod. 'Sure, don't worry about it. I'll collect the twins if you're running behind.'

Harry gave a grateful smile and, as he left, Juan told him that he would be there in a moment.

'So, this is the new assertive Cate?' Juan smiled.

'I can be assertive when it's required.'

'I know that,' Juan said, recalling how Cate had stood up to the director of nursing on Harry's behalf.

'I could make a stand today and tell him that I won't pick up the twins,' Cate said, 'but the fact is this place needs new consultants more than it needs me to get away on time, and if watching Harry's children for fifteen minutes facilitates that...'

'I lied,' Juan interrupted Cate, to tell her the real reason that he was there. 'It would have been just as easy to deal with the health insurance forms online.' He looked into her serious eyes and loathed having hurt her. 'I hated how we ended things the other day,' Juan admitted. 'It was supposed to be fun, it was supposed to be...' He didn't know how best to explain it. 'It wasn't supposed to end like that.'

She gave a watery smile. 'I know Sunday was a difficult day for you.'

'That was the reason I chose to take myself far away,' Juan explained. 'The last place I thought I'd be was in Emergency, being looked after by you. I overreacted.'

'I can understand why.' Cate gave a smile. 'How's the house-sharing?'

Juan rolled his eyes. 'Awful,' he admitted. 'I think I am maybe too old to share, they are getting on my nerves.' He didn't tell her Nurse Purple Face was sulking from his lack of advances, or how he had stayed in for two nights in a row for the first time since his arrival in Australia. Neither did he tell her just how much he wanted to see her again, so they could end things better.

'Are you going to watch the skydive on Sunday?' Juan asked.

Cate shook her head and then shrugged. 'I don't know,' she admitted. 'Kelly wanted me to go along for moral support but...' She was blinking back threatening tears, could not stand the thought of saying goodbye to him in a crowd, on another wild night out. It was perhaps better here, in her office, alone with him.

'Do you want to keep in touch?' Juan offered. 'I tried to look you up on the internet...'

'I changed my privacy settings,' Cate admitted. She could not stand the thought of keeping in touch with him, of watching his life from a distance. She could not imagine keeping up the pretence of being mere friends who'd had a thing going once, however briefly. 'I think we should just leave it as it is. It was fun.'

There was nothing fun about how she was feeling but she tried to keep things light.

'I brought you a present,' Juan said.

'Bought.' Cate smiled.

'No, brought,' Juan said, and went into his bag. It was perhaps the strangest present she had ever received and one only he could give. 'I made it for you before I left the apartment. I was cleaning out the fridge...' It was a huge jar of *chimichurri* and Cate had this vision of her dividing it up into freezer bags, sustaining the memory of Juan with one tiny taste each Sunday.

'Thank you.'

'I have to go. I need to speak to Harry. I never did get around to it.'

'You're not going to discuss the children?'

'Of course I am,' Juan said. 'I told you that I would.'

'But you can't...'

'I have dealt with colleagues,' he said. 'In another life, I was quite a demanding boss.'

'I can't imagine it.'

'I know,' Juan said. 'So...' He gave her a smile and pulled her into his arms, a sort of big-brother hug that lasted about a third of a second because she just melted against him. His touch was so fierce that she was at risk

of breaking down and breaking the rules and admitting
the heartbreak he was going to cause her.

'Please, don't say, "This could be it,"' Cate said.

'I won't,' Juan said, 'because it is.'

'You could come for dinner...' She could not stand
to say goodbye like this, didn't want it to be a quick hi
and bye in her office. They may not have counted for
much but surely they counted for more than that. 'No
big deal...' She pulled back, forced a smile. 'My neighbours will probably be there, it would just be nice to
say goodbye properly.'

'It would,' Juan said, and his smile was slightly
wicked. 'You know, though, that it will end in bed?'

'I would hope so if I have to cook.'

A two-night stand was surely better than one?

She gave him her address, signed over her heart to
the certainty of more misery for the sake of tonight, but
it would be worth it one day, Cate hoped. And, despite
saying it was no big deal now, Cate, who never planned
her meals, had to suddenly plan dinner!

'Bridgette?' Cate winced a bit as she called in a favour from her neighbour and friend, because it involved
shopping and lighting a barbeque and putting dinner on.
Oh, and could she also get wine and beer...?

'Anything else?' She could tell Bridgette was smiling.

'I can't ask.'

'You want me to make your bed, don't you?'

'And maybe a little tidy?' Cate cringed.

'So long as I get to meet the man I'm cooking and
cleaning for!'

Cate hung up the phone, smiling. It was nice to have
friends you could lean on, nice to have people who you

had enough history with that you could call on at times like this—she wondered how Juan managed without them. She wondered how he functioned in a world without that team, people who stepped in for the big and the little without question. She headed out of her office and passed Harry's office, where a couple of people sat waiting outside to be interviewed. As she did so, she silently thanked Juan for the forced introspection.

Cate knew what she wanted now—to be a part of a team, to be a part of the back-up, not to be finding solutions to a problem that she didn't think was one.

Cate walked up to Admin and knocked on Lillian's office.

'Cate!' Lillian looked up. 'I was just about to email you. We've sorted out the interview times.'

'Actually, that's what I wanted to discuss.' Cate took a deep breath. 'I'm withdrawing my application.'

'Cate?'

'I'll stay on till you find someone suitable, of course. I'm going to have a think, but I might resign as Associate. I want to get back to nursing.'

'You're a good manager, Cate.'

'Maybe,' Cate said, 'but I think I'm a better nurse.' She shook her head. 'It's just not for me.'

CHAPTER FIFTEEN

PERHAPS THE BIKE accident combined with the anniversary had unsettled him more than he'd realised, Juan thought as he stepped off the train that evening and walked in the direction of Cate's house. Saying goodbye had always been easy until now—it had always been about having fun, living life and then moving on.

And he would move on, Juan told himself. So too would Cate, he thought with a wry smile as he knocked at her front door and there was no answer.

She wasn't even home.

Juan had never been stood up and wondered if maybe she had just changed her mind or, more logically, she had been caught up at work, minding Harry's kids—then he heard the sound of laughter coming from the back of the house.

'Cate?' Juan peered over the gate. She was sitting at an outdoor table, dressed in shorts and that black halterneck and looking completely relaxed, smiling and laughing with a friend as she turned to him.

'Juan?' Cate gave a wide smile. 'Were you knocking? I should have said—if I'm outside, just come through the gate.' Cate walked over and unlatched it. 'Sorry, I never thought. Everyone knows…'

Everyone who was in her life, Juan thought, handing her a bottle of wine and taking in the gorgeous fragrance of meat cooking on the barbeque.

'This is Bridgette, my neighbour,' Cate introduced them. 'She came over to borrow an egg!'

'An hour ago,' Bridgette said, unashamedly looking Juan up and down.

Juan smiled and saw the nuts and the bottle of champagne on the table and, no, Cate hadn't been nervously awaiting his arrival—her world would carry on just fine without him.

'I'll leave you to it.' Bridgette went to stand.

'Don't go on my account,' Juan said.

Bridgette didn't need to be asked twice; she sat down again as Cate went to offer Juan a drink and then realised she needed a glass.

'I can get it,' Juan said, and held up his bottle of wine. 'Shall I put this in the fridge?'

'Please.'

As he walked through to the kitchen, Bridgette's eyes widened and her mouth gaped as she looked at Cate. 'Oh, my word!' she mouthed.

'Told you.'

'I've never considered a foursome till now.' Bridgette winked, making Cate laugh out loud.

Juan could hear the laughter coming from the garden. It was the strangest feeling, stepping into Cate's home—it was just that, a home. To the right were two sofas piled high with cushions and in the centre a coffee table brimmed with magazines. There were bookshelves, which was something he hadn't seen in a while, and he would have loved to browse but he saved that for the fridge! Smiling, he opened it and saw the contents were those of a busy single woman who didn't have much time to cook.

Yes, it was a home but more than that it was *her* home.

It was almost as if Juan recognised it.

It was a lovely evening. James, Bridgette's husband, came home from work and must have heard the laughter and known about the gate too, because he came straight from the car to Cate's garden.

Juan wanted time alone with Cate, yet he wanted this as well. For, somehow, this way he knew her more.

It was nice to pause, to enjoy the end of summer.

'There's a cool change coming tonight.' Bridgette fanned herself as Cate went over and lifted the lid on the barbeque and checked dinner.

'Your skydive might be rained off.' Cate smiled at Juan.

'No, it is forecast to be fine again for the weekend,' Juan said. 'Are you sure you won't change your mind?'

'Cate, skydiving?' Bridgette laughed. 'James had to come and change the light bulb on her staircase a few weeks ago!' Bridgette drained her drink and went to stand. 'Now we really do have to go.'

'Stay,' Cate offered, as Juan took up the knife and started to carve. Her offer was more out of habit than politeness. 'There's plenty.'

'I'll leave you two...'

'It's not a romantic dinner for two.' Cate grinned, trying to keep up the pretence for just a little while longer, trying to keep things casual for just one more night.

'James has to ring his mum,' Bridgette said as James frowned. 'It's her birthday.'

'Oh, God, so it is!' James suddenly stood.

'Take some lamb if you want, save you cooking,' Cate offered.

Juan had sliced the lamb in a way Cate would never have—thin slivers instead of her usual rather messy effort, and it looked somehow elegant. Bridgette licked her lips.

'Yes, please.'

She gave them some jacket potatoes too and a plate with the mango salad Bridgette had prepared.

'It's normally Bridgette and James feeding me,' Cate explained as she loaded the plates.

'Yes, you're not exactly known for your cooking skills.' Bridgette said. And then there was the most terribly awkward bit. 'It was lovely meeting you, Juan. Next time…' And Bridgette hesitated. 'Well, it was lovely meeting you.'

'Same here,' Juan said, and gave her a kiss then shook James's hand.

'They seem really nice,' Juan said when it was just the two of them.

'They are.' Cate nodded. 'Bridgette knows when I need tissues and when I need champagne bubbles!' She met his eyes. 'I just withdrew my application for the nurse unit manager's job.'

Juan gave a wry smile. For a moment there, he had thought the tissues or bubbles had been about him. 'How come?' he asked.

'I don't want to talk about it.'

'Why?'

'Because…' She blew a breath upwards that made a strand of hair lift on her forehead. 'Because I just spent nearly an hour going over it with Bridgette and…'

'She'll still be here next week?' Juan finished for her.

Cate nodded.

'You know…' Juan smiled. 'I've got addicted to day-time soaps while I've been here. If I miss a couple of episodes I can soon catch up. I love watching it when I wake up from a night shift. I can't believe I'm not going to find out what happened to the baby…'

Cate laughed.

'And I can't believe I'm not going to know what happens with you.'

It was the closest either of them had come to admitting how hard this was.

'Well, you're not going to find me with a clipboard as the director of nursing in a couple of years,' Cate said. 'I've just shot my career in the foot.'

'If it changes anything, I did speak to Harry,' Juan said. 'Things should improve there.'

'It's not just Harry. I haven't been as happy as I should be at work for quite some time now. That's why I was thinking about being a paramedic. I've been try-ing to sort out what I wanted, what was wrong, and when I actually sat down and really thought about it I realised I've only been unsettled since I started climbing the ranks. I know what I love, being a nurse in Emer-gency, and so that's what I'm going to do.'

'Good for you.'

'I might regret that choice when I get my pay cheque,' Cate sighed. 'And I might regret it again when the new manager starts. I think they're going to be pretty rig-orous about who they choose.' She gave a shrug. 'Not my problem any more.'

It was such a bitter-sweet night.

Never had she laughed so much as he tried to teach her to tango and never had he relished more the sensual movement, the feel of a woman in his arms, the touch of another person and the ability to simply move.

To climb the stairs and see for the first time her bedroom. To have fingers that moved and could untie the knot of her halterneck—he took not a second of it for granted.

'I am going to leave you money by the bed.' Juan smiled as he undressed her. 'Not for the sex but for a new top…'

He made her laugh. 'It's my Juan top, the rest are…' Paul's name did not belong in this room any more, the only name that would be uttered here was Juan's.

She felt his mouth on her shoulder.

'You are over him?' Juan checked, and then made slow love to her.

Yes, she was over Paul, so much more than he knew. Now she just had to get over Juan.

'The reason I didn't just leave it at sex…' Juan spoke to the darkness as they both tried to sleep later, answering the bitter questions she had hurled that night '…is because I care about you and what happens. If things were—'

'Please, don't,' Cate interrupted. 'I don't want to hear that if things were different we might have made it. I don't want to think how it might have been if we'd had more time, because…' It was as simple as that—his visa ran out next week. 'We don't.'

CHAPTER SIXTEEN

JUAN WOKE AT TWO.

He was on his back, Cate curled up in a ball by his side. He could hear the rumble of thunder in the distance and, as always, he moved his hands and then his feet…

Just to check.

He wondered if it would disturb Cate if he went downstairs and made a drink, perhaps put on the television. He didn't even have a book with him to read.

'What was it like?'

Her question filled the darkness; he was glad she did not turn. The psychologist on the spinal unit had asked on many occasions and the nurses had been amazing, but he'd answered them all correctly and just kept it all in.

By day.

Martina certainly hadn't wanted to know and his parents and family he had not wanted to burden.

Cate didn't see it like that.

'You really want to know?' he said to the darkness.

'I do.'

'Stay there,' he said, and Cate screwed her eyes closed and did not turn to him.

'It was very busy,' Juan said. 'For the first few days

there are tests and Theatre and endless examinations and equipment and you keep waiting for things to change. Everyone is waiting for news, for updates and progress and it really has not sunk in. I had my fracture stabilised and it was wait and see. I had severe spinal swelling so they were unsure of the extent of the damage. I tried to stay positive for Martina and my family but I wasn't feeling positive at all,' Juan explained. 'I knew, almost as soon as I hit the pavement, that I had broken my neck.' He closed his eyes for a moment before carrying on. 'I did not believe that anything the surgeon could do would help.'

'You thought that was it.'

'Completely,' Juan said. 'All the tests, the tentative diagnosis, my family trying to keep positive, I went along with it for them, but in my heart I was sure it was permanent.'

'Were you scared?'

'You are too busy to be scared,' Juan said. 'The day is full. You start at six with obs and a drink, then breakfast, then wash, then doctors' rounds, then physio, visitors, more physio, exercises every hour...' He listed the day. 'Then at about ten you are settled and perhaps watch a movie. I used to sleep with the television on, but someone would turn it off and I used to wake...' He hesitated. 'You really want to hear this?'

'Yes.'

He told her about the nights.

Finally, he told somebody about the nights. How it felt to be trapped in only your head, how every missed opportunity, every wasted moment taunted, how the simplest things mattered in a way that they never had before.

'Every hour the nurses come around, day and night, and you have passive exercise. They move your limbs, your ankles, your hands. One of the nurses was trying to chat to Martina, trying to show her how she could move my fingers and wrists.' He lifted his index finger and thumb and, unseen by Cate, started pulling them together and then apart. '"That might mean he can hold a cup," the nurse told Martina, "or do up a shirt." And then she showed Martina how to turn my wrist in the hope I could one day have a drink by myself, and I saw her face…'

'Was she overwhelmed?'

'She couldn't do it,' Juan said. 'I saw her expression and when the nurse had gone she broke down.'

Then he told Cate about the night only three others knew about.

Because they had lain there in silence as they'd heard it.

'"I can't do this, Juan…" Martina couldn't even look me in the eye to tell me; instead she sat down by the bed.

'"It will be okay," I said.

'"When?"

'I just lay there. I'd have loved to know that answer too.

'"It's not what I envisaged, Juan. When you asked me to marry you, when I said yes, this was not how I planned things to be."' He'd hated how she'd attempted a joke. '"You always said that I would be a terrible nurse."

'"I don't want you to be my nurse."'

Cate listened as he told her some more of Martina's words, how worried she was about what others might think about her leaving him while he faced a future in a wheelchair.

'I told her that I would always say it was by mutual agreement and I would have stuck to that, except she calls me now. Martina has a different recollection of our conversation. She says she was in shock, that she just needed some time to adjust...'

Cate swallowed, wondered if it was pride holding him back from returning to Martina, but Juan shook his head when she asked him.

'I know, had I not got better, that I would never have seen Martina again.'

He told her how slowly, so slowly, sensations had started to come back. How it had hurt when they did, first his arms and then later his wrists. Then his thighs and slowly his calves and feet. 'I did the rehab, I dragged myself to physio, I learnt to walk, and then she started to visit. Martina had decided that maybe we could work through it, that maybe I did need her help after all. I needed her long before that,' Juan said. 'I certainly don't need her now. I flew to Australia. We were going to come here for our honeymoon but I came by myself. I was very thin and weak when I got here, but I spent months building my body up.'

Cate knew she had been right.

She had known so little about him.

'Martina wants it to go back to the way it was.'

'It can't?'

'No,' Juan said, 'because something like that is life-altering. You don't go back to how you were. When something that big happens, you find out who you really are...'

'And you are?'

'I'm still finding out,' Juan said. 'But I'm not the person I once was.'

She understood that.

Cate lay in the silence, listening to his breathing, and, even though it was nowhere near as severe as what had happened to him, Cate felt she had been through something life-changing. Juan had changed her. She couldn't go back to how she had been.

'I'm a different person now,' Juan said.

So too was she.

So different.

Cate woke to a sound that was unfamiliar—rain was beating against the window, heavy rain that was so needed. She thought of the firefighters and how thankful they would be for the reprieve, and the homeowners who had lived under the shadow of imminent danger for weeks now.

The threat had passed.

Just as Juan would soon move on.

All the attempts to safeguard her heart had been in vain and in a little while she would be doing what she most dreaded and saying goodbye to him.

She turned and looked over to the sight of Juan sleeping and smiled because she'd never thought she'd find the spill of long black hair on her pillow sexy, or that her toes might curl at what was now more than a few days' growth—he officially had a beard!

And she'd never thought she'd be so bold as to move over and start to kiss his flat nipples.

More than that she'd never felt so *inclined*, or had wanted another so much.

He felt her lips on his chest and he lay there; he

felt her mouth over his nipples and her tongue and he closed his eyes.

Juan loved sex, preferably quick. Hot, passionate sex was how things had had to be, not lying there with a mouth exploring, working its way down his stomach. He felt her hands move along his thighs, sensations returning, flooding his body, the slow burn of making love and being made love to.

He felt her hand grip his shaft, felt lips start to explore him, and for a second he wanted to stop her for, as it had in the hospital, sometimes feelings hurt as they returned.

Her mouth was hot and intimate and he moaned in pleasure and gave in to her.

Cate felt his hands in her hair, the gentle guidance of his palm. So many things had changed since Juan had come into her life—she could explore without shame and taste without guilt, just let herself live in the moment, for this moment at least.

He tasted of both him and of her, and she heard his ragged moan as she kissed him deeper, taking him further, and Juan gave in then.

The shout was primal and it came from somewhere he had never been.

She felt the jerk and the rush at the back of her throat and she was coming just from feeling him, from tasting him.

From adoring him.

CHAPTER SEVENTEEN

'STAY THERE,' JUAN said as the alarm blared like a siren. 'I'll bring us coffee.'

It was stupid to lie there and listen to him in her kitchen for the first time and to think she could miss something that had only happened once.

She was very close to crying and absolutely determined not to.

He brought her coffee and they drank it in strained silence. Juan headed off to the shower and then came out and dressed. He sat on the bed and she watched him pulling on his boots for the first and last time.

He made every moment matter.

'It's good to hear the rain.'

'It is,' Cate said. 'I'll be told off now for ordering too many burn packs.'

'Better too many than not enough,' Juan said. 'I think you made the right choice about work.'

Cate nodded, she didn't trust herself to speak.

'I'd better go,' Juan said, when it was clear she was struggling. 'I start at eight…'

'Sure.'

'Thank you for last night, for all our times…'

'Go,' Cate said, 'or I'm going to fail…'

'Fail what?'

'Living in the moment, not getting too involved.'

'Will you be okay?'

'Of course, as long as I avoid any tall Argentinian doctors that happen to be passing through...'

'No regrets?'

'No.' Cate shook her head. 'I don't think so anyway. You?'

'Potentially,' Juan said. 'Will you be there on Sunday?'

'No...' Cate shook her head, she couldn't put herself through this again, but a part of her couldn't stand never to see him again. 'I don't know.'

He kissed her again but it didn't quite work out and he stood. 'I'm going to go.' She went to get up, to see him out.

'Stay there,' Juan said.

So she did.

Hearing the door close hurt a million times more than it ever had.

Cate did get up. She stood back from the window, watched him walk in the direction of the train station.

She knew then what she'd been scared of right from the very start—not the one night with him, not the casual aspect. It was this part she'd been dreading, and the next part and the next.

Juan did not look back.

He felt the rain on his face and he loved it, loved living, loved the freedom. It was time to move on, he told himself.

He took the train to the city and watched as a young woman in a wheelchair boarded and gave him a dark look as she caught him staring.

'Excuse me,' Juan said. He did not look away and

maybe their souls recognised each other because they got talking, so much so that Juan was going to be late for his final shift in Australia. He was sitting at a train station, having a coffee, when his new friend told him a truth.

'Maybe it's time to go home, Juan, and face things,' she suggested. 'Maybe it's time to stop running away.'

'I think it is.'

He was only ten minutes late for work and no one seemed to notice. He walked around the unit with Paddy taking the handover then told him he hoped that he had a good weekend.

'Jason!' Juan looked down at his very drowsy patient. 'Do you remember me?'

'Of course he does,' Lisa said. 'Jason, it's Juan, the doctor who brought you here.'

He saw Jason's eyes flicker open.

'You've had a rough time, haven't you, my friend?' Jason had gone downhill a few days after his admission and had been intubated two days ago. They were trying now to extubate him.

Juan looked over at Jason's mother and saw Lisa's eyes brimming with tears. 'We're hoping he finally gets the tube out today.'

'It will happen when it's ready,' Juan said. 'You will have heard the saying—difficult intubations mean difficult extubations. We expect this…'

Lisa nodded.

'We just want him home.'

There was that word again.

'He will be,' Juan assured her. 'It makes it no easier on you but this is, for Jason, normal.' Juan sat on the bed with his young friend. 'We're going to let the sedation wear off this morning and see how his breathing goes, and if he's keeping his saturations then we'll think about removing the tube later today.'

'Will you be here?'

'I'm on till tomorrow evening,' Juan said. 'We'll get through this.'

'Then you're off. To New Zealand, isn't it? Or so I've heard,' Lisa said.

'I'm not sure...' Juan looked up as Kent came over.

'You're popular this morning,' Kent said. 'I've just taken a couple of calls for you. I said I didn't know if you were working today but that I'd find out and pass the message on if you were.'

They were so much more efficient here than at Bayside!

'Thanks,' Juan said to Kent, and then looked at the note. He grimaced when he read it and then put it in his pocket.

'So, you're not sure about New Zealand?' Lisa resumed the conversation.

'Nope,' Juan said. 'I think it might be time for home.'

He gave Jason's shoulder a squeeze and told him he'd be back to check in on him in a little while. He went out to the on-call room to make a couple of calls that he'd been putting off for way too long now.

'Martina.' He was kind, he was firm and there was no arguing with someone who had made up their mind. 'You need to stop calling me.'

They spoke for a little while and as Juan went to end the call she asked him a question.

'Can we at least be friends?'

Juan was about to say no, because he didn't need the

constant reminders, but perhaps that did not matter any more—maybe they could be.

'Some day perhaps,' Juan answered.

He rang off, but sat there for a very long time with the phone still in his hand. He understood fully why Cate couldn't stand to catch up with him on social media, how it would hurt to watch someone's life from a distance.

Martina didn't hurt any more.

He wasn't just letting go of a love that had once been, he was letting go too of the man that he'd once been. All the dreams and aspirations, even thoughts, that had existed were alien to Juan now.

The old Juan was gone and it almost hurt to finally let go, but there was a sense of relief when he did.

He *was* a different person.

A wiser person.

A happy person.

A good man.

The second phone call Juan had expected to be the tough one—but it turned out to be the most straightforward decision in his life.

He wanted to go home.

CHAPTER EIGHTEEN

SOON SHE WOULD have no regrets, Cate told herself.

In a few weeks from now, surely it wouldn't hurt so much?

Cate fervently wished that she could do the casual relationship thing, wished that she hadn't had to go and fall quite so hard. Walking to the shops on Saturday morning, Cate looked up at the rainbow that had come out, telling herself it meant something. She was determined to buy a delicious top with the money she'd found on the hall table after he'd gone.

No, it hadn't offended; instead, it had made her smile.

Cate wasn't smiling now.

Tears were precariously close and she could see Kelly coming out of the boutique. The last thing Cate wanted now was conversation and she turned to look into a shop window, hoping that Kelly wouldn't notice her.

It was an antique shop and Cate looked at the rings, her eyes catching sight of a bevelled silver one with an amethyst and she walked inside.

'Can I look at a ring in the window?' Cate pointed it out and the assistant chatted as she headed over to fetch it.

'It just went in the window this morning.' The assistant smiled as she handed it over and as Cate looked, there inside she saw the words she really needed to see, and she thanked Elsie and her lover for them.

Je t'adore.

Cate thanked the wonderful old woman who had given her that push to live a little more, as she wanted, rather than how she felt she should. She thanked too the man who had made her feel more adored than she ever had.

It wasn't an impulse buy, it was an essential buy, and as she handed over the money he had left, yes, it came from Juan.

'Cate!' Kelly saw her coming out of the antique store. 'What are you up to?'

'Shopping.' Cate was getting good at forcing that smile. 'Ready for your jump tomorrow?'

'I can't wait,' Kelly smiled. 'You should come.'

'I might come along and watch.' Cate wondered if it would just make things worse, but the chance of seeing him again, even the sight of him hurtling out of a plane, was surely better than not seeing him at all.

'I meant you should come and jump.'

'It's too late now, the bookings are all done.'

Kelly shook her head. 'There's a spot that's opened up. It's all paid for—it was too late for a refund.'

Cate twisted the ring on her finger and made the second most foolish choice of her life.

'I'll jump,' Cate said, terrified not just at the prospect of leaping out of a plane but at the thought of seeing Juan again and having to say goodbye—again. 'But I can't just take someone's place without paying. Who do I owe?'

'Juan.' Kelly said, and Cate simply stood as Juan

moved out of her life for ever, just as she had always known that he would one day. 'He said he'd been looking forward to it but had somewhere he needed to be. I think he's already gone.'

Cate made it home without crying and when there was a knock at the door she forced that smile and saw that it was Bridgette.

'Thanks so much for your help the other day,' Cate said.

'It was no big deal. I brought back your plates.' She handed them to Cate. 'The lamb was delicious.'

'Thanks to you.'

'So was Juan!'

'I know,' Cate said. 'He's gone to New Zealand…' She tried to sound upbeat. 'I knew all along he would, it was just…' She couldn't finish, couldn't pretend that it wasn't agony for even a second longer.

'Do you want…?' Bridgette stood there. By now Cate usually would have opened the door and invited her in. 'Do you want company?'

'No, thanks.' Cate shook her head.

'If you do?'

'I know,' Cate said, closing the door, her eyes so full of tears that as she walked into the kitchen she faltered and tripped and the plates crashed to the floor.

Yes, she could have broken her neck.

As easily as that.

She stared at the mess and then the tears fell.

It hadn't been a fling or a holiday romance, neither had it even been a rebound.

It was love and she'd lost it.

CHAPTER NINETEEN

CATE FELT MORE than a pang of guilt for the lecture she'd delivered to Juan about being reckless to even consider the skydive. There was a disabled group jumping before the emergency team and Cate knew that she should have got her facts straight before accusing him of being careless.

But, then, she hadn't been thinking very straight at the time and, really—a motorbike?

Then she thought of Juan riding through the hills, the elation he must have felt, and still felt each day over and over again, as he chose to live his life the way he wanted to, and she smiled for him instead.

'You need to take that ring off,' the instructor told her, and Cate pulled it off and pocketed it, having visions of it knotting in the strings as she jumped into the sky.

'Are you okay?' Kelly asked through chattering teeth.

'I've never been more scared in my life,' Cate admitted. 'Tell me, why am I doing this again?'

'For a good cause?' Kelly offered as, instructions over, they walked towards the plane. Kelly wasn't looking quite so confident now.

'I'm sorry I pushed you into this, Cate,' Kelly said. 'I'm petrified.'

It came as little comfort to know she wasn't the only one as she sat with her fellow suicide and the plane rose into the sky.

Kelly went first. She left the plane screaming. Abby went second and one by one the rest followed.

Cate was last, which was so much worse in so many ways—there were no friends to bolster her, no one to watch her shame as she said, no, she couldn't do it.

'I can't,' she said, as she was strapped to her sky-diver. 'I've changed my mind.'

'All you have to remember is to lift your legs as we land.'

'I can't.'

'Cate…' The instructor was more than used to this, but when over and over Cate insisted that, no, this really wasn't what she wanted, he was about to relent and unstrap her.

'You'll regret it if you don't,' he warned her.

Cate had heard something like that somewhere before.

'I'll do it.'

The instructor took the small window but, even if he hadn't, now Cate's mind was made up there would be no changing it.

That much she knew about herself.

There was no feeling like it.

Even with her eyes closed, even pretending she wasn't really doing it, there was nothing, Cate quickly found out, like it in the world.

She screamed and screamed as she opened her eyes to a world that was amazing. The sky and the bay were dressed in vivid blues as far as the eye could see. Then she saw the white chop of the waves on the back beaches and the calm stillness of the bay, felt the pressure of the air, and Cate knew why she was doing this now.

I'm doing this for me.

She was doing it for the exhilaration of jumping out of a plane and feeling the pressure and the surprisingly strong cushion of thin air, for the fear and the fun and the uncertainty that all too often she had refused to embrace.

But finally she had.

Cate felt the chute jerk and the freefall break, and she thought about Juan, understood his need to embrace things, to experience and to fully sample the world. Floating above the tea trees, it happened then, just as Elsie had said it would—her heart soared for him.

'Juan!' Kelly turned. Still giddy from jumping, she smiled when she saw who it was. 'I didn't recognise you.'

'I figured it was time for a haircut,' Juan said. 'I wanted to come and watch the jumping but I am later getting here than I thought I would be.' His eyes scanned the gathering, hoping to get a glimpse of Cate; he had been to her home but she wasn't there and he had hoped she might have come along to give her colleagues moral support, but there was no sign of her.

'We're going out for dinner afterwards,' Kelly said.

Juan gave a noncommittal nod. 'How was your jump?' he asked her.

'It was the scariest moment of my life,' Kelly admitted. 'I feel terrible for pushing Cate into it, though

I don't think she'll jump. She was pea green the last time I saw her.'

'Cate's jumping?'

'There she is!' Kelly shouted, and Juan looked up, watched the two figures jumping out of a plane, and he grinned, for he'd known there was a wild side to her.

'Who'd have thought?' Kelly said as Cate's screams and laughter came into earshot.

Me, Juan said silently, because he'd seen a different side to her, the untapped spirit that lay inside and the quiet strength too. He could only smile that she wasn't crying or miserable, though his ego would have liked a slightly more subdued Cate after he had seemingly left.

No, he wouldn't, Juan decided as he watched her land, heard her laughing as she untangled herself and then, dusting down her legs, she walked to the group.

'That was amazing!' Cate shouted. 'I can't believe I'm saying this but I want to do it....' Then her voice halted as she looked at the group of colleagues and friends and saw that Juan was amongst them.

A different Juan because that long shock of black hair had been cut. She'd loved his hair, yet he looked incredible with it shorter too. And what was with the clean-shaven jaw?

'I thought you were in New Zealand!' She tried to hide her exhilaration; she didn't want her colleagues knowing what had gone on between them, but the unexpected sight of him was more breathtaking than jumping out of a plane.

'So did everyone.' Juan grinned.

'You've had a haircut!'

He nodded.

'How was it?'

Juan pulled her aside. She knew him, knew the big deal it must have been, and he told her the truth. 'Can you believe I broke into a sweat as I walked in?'

'Yes.'

'The girl must have been all of eighteen and could not have been more bored as she cut my hair. "What did you do to your neck?" she asked when she saw the scar.'

'What did you say?' Cate smiled at grey eyes she had thought she might never see again.

'That I went to get a haircut.' Juan grinned. 'She did not get the joke, of course. I think she thought my English was no good.'

'So how come you finally got it cut?'

'My gap year is over,' Juan said. 'It is time to get to work.' He saw her frown. 'Harry rang me at the children's hospital on Friday and said that he had found only one applicant suitable and that they really needed two. He said that he wanted me to work at Bayside. The applications have to be in Personnel by Monday and, given I was working till last night, this morning was our only chance for a formal interview.'

'For a three-month contract?'

'No.' They started walking towards the crowd, who were calling to them to get a move on. 'For a permanent role.'

Cate blinked, because seeing Juan every day was going to be hard. Yes, she knew they had something, should be pleased they didn't have a clock hanging over them now, but to get closer to him, to have to work alongside him...

'I might have to go to New Zealand while the applications are sorted. Harry is going to try and help to sort things with Immigration but we will have to see what happens.' Then he stopped walking and caught her hand and turned her to face him. 'Marry me?' He said it just like that, walking towards the shed where all their colleagues were. 'I was going to ask that we take things more seriously, that we see how things work out, but I already know what I want.'

'Marriage?' She looked at him. 'For a visa?'

'Cate.' He held her eyes. 'Ask yourself that question again. Why do you think I want this job, why do you think I want to be here?'

'Me?'

'You,' Juan said. 'We can live here or in Argentina, or...' He looked at her. 'I don't care. I just don't want to be apart from you. I take marriage seriously, and today I watched you jump out of that plane and, yes, like anyone, I had some concerns. If something terrible had happened, I would have been there. I knew it as truth as I watched you fall. I knew too that if something happened, you would be the first to say we have only been with each other a little while, it is not serious, that I don't have to hang around...'

She could feel tears stinging the back of her throat as he continued.

'I want the good and bad, in sickness and in health, and I want them with you.'

It wasn't a game.

The feelings she had been fighting, glimpsing, scorning herself for feeling had been real after all.

'Do I have to ask twice?' Juan said, and she shook her head.

'That's a yes,' Cate said, and it was hardly even a decision because it needed no thought when her heart knew the answer.

'I should warn you,' Juan said. 'I'm guaranteed to have a limp when I'm older.'

'I'll buy you a cane.' Cate smiled, and her heart swelled as she glimpsed the truth. They had a future, one where his black hair would go silver and he wasn't temporary but was there with her, for all of it. It was overwhelming, more overwhelming than jumping out of a plane, more exhilarating than freefalling.

'We're going shopping,' Juan said.

'Shopping?'

'For a ring.'

She caught his hand. 'I've already bought the ring, or rather you have.'

'What?' He half smiled and frowned as she took a silver ring out of her pocket and handed it to him. He turned it over and over in vague recognition.

'I used the money you left for me to get a top on this instead. It was Elsie's,' Cate explained. 'I found it in an antique shop in the village.'

He looked at the silver ring in his hand and read the inscription and then he looked at her, a woman who didn't want diamonds, who wanted only his love.

'*Je t'adore*,' Juan said, and took her right hand. 'We don't have separate engagement rings in Argentina, so this is your wedding band,' he told her. 'It is worn on the right hand till our wedding day,' he explained, slipping the ring on her finger, and it fitted perfectly. It was absolutely meant to be.

She could hear the screams and shouts from Kelly and Abby as Juan bent over and kissed her in full view of everyone. Readily, Cate kissed him back.

'They'll want us to go out and celebrate when we tell them,' Cate warned, as they started running over.

'No,' Juan said, and he thought about the friend he had made on the train, about the conversation that, since he had met Cate, had been running through his mind. He recalled the feeling of stepping into her house and hearing the sound of her laughter from the garden. 'We are going back to yours. It's time for me to stop running away.'

Juan took her hand in his. 'We're going home.'

CHAPTER TWENTY

'I AM SO glad to be out of that place for four weeks.'

They were high above the clouds, on their way to Argentina to get married. Cate's family was coming out next week, but for now Cate and Juan were sitting sipping champagne. Cate felt guilty that Juan had got business-class tickets and it was nice to be grumbling about work but, in truth, to be happy at work, too. The new nurse unit manager had started and was making very sure that Cate knew who was boss. 'Marnie's awful.' Cate sighed. 'I don't think she understands that I resigned rather than that I was demoted and that I have absolutely no desire to do her job.'

'I like her,' Juan said.

'You like Marnie?'

'I do.' Juan shrugged. 'The place is running well. She's very strict and she takes no nonsense and Marnie's certainly stopped all the carry-on with Harry and his children.'

'Leave Harry alone,' Cate said.

'No. If something happened to you, would you want me dragging our baby in at four a.m.?'

'No,' Cate admitted. 'But we don't have a baby and—'

'We could,' Juan interrupted.

'Isn't it too soon?'

'Not for me,' Juan said. He'd seen the look in her eyes last night when Bridgette had told them she and James were expecting a baby.

Cate looked at him. Sometimes she had to pinch herself, sometimes she actually jumped when she walked into the house and he was still there.

'You were supposed to be a one-night stand,' Cate said. 'My wild fling. And now, here we are, talking about babies.'

'You don't do wild flings,' Juan said.

'I know.'

He sat as she contemplated the future. Cate was the least impulsive person he knew, but when she made her mind up, she made it up—he'd realised that.

'Next year,' Cate said. 'I want a year of just us and getting to know each other and being as happy as we are. Anyway,' Cate said, 'we need to save for it. I've just had my first full pay since I demoted myself.' She gave a small wince. 'And you've blown your savings flying my family out for the wedding and you've only just started back at work full time.'

'Whenever you're ready,' Juan said and he looked over. There was so much to learn, so much to know and so much that hadn't mattered to Cate that had mattered to so many others.

As they approached Buenos Aires some time later, Cate woke up and saw a pensive Juan looking out of the window, staring down at his home town. He only stopped when the flight attendant told him to close the shutter for landing.

'Nervous?' Cate asked.

'Not for myself,' Juan admitted. 'I never thought I

would be so ready to go back. I just wonder how they are going to react to me.' He gave her a smile. 'To the new Juan.'

They loved him.

All his family were there at the airport—as unconventional and as glamorous and as exotic as Juan. They welcomed Cate with open arms and it wasn't just blood family who were there to greet him on his return.

'This is Eduard,' Juan introduced them, and Cate hugged him as fiercely as Juan had. 'And this is Felicia…'

'We are so excited,' Felicia said. 'My English is crap.'

'I taught her,' Juan said.

'Of course you did.'

'We are so excited,' Ramona, his mother, told her as they drove towards their home. 'Pardon my crap English.'

Cate started to laugh. 'You have to tell them what they're saying,' she said to Juan.

'But I love it too much to spoil it,' Juan said.

They chatted about the plans for the wedding and the menu. Their English was littered with the swear words Juan had told them were the words Cate would want to hear.

'It sounds wonderful,' Cate said to the blue air, even though she had no idea what the dishes that were being talked about were.

'Wow!' Cate looked out of the window the whole ride from the airport and she had said it often. Buenos Aires was such a busy, vibrant city, a lot like the man it had produced, yet there was incredible elegance too.

'I was expecting fields and horses.'

'This is Recoleta,' Juan explained. 'We are nearly at

my parents'.' Cate swallowed as they drove down the very affluent streets. The houses were amazing, the streets lined with trees and golden streetlights. 'There is Medicina,' Juan explained, 'where I studied medicine…and over there is the best dance school. You have to learn the tango before the wedding.'

'Please!'

'You do. I have booked you for lessons, and over there…' her head turned to where he was pointing '…is where we will be having our celebration.'

He watched as Cate's jaw gaped. It was the most beautiful restaurant and she cringed when she thought of the cost, worried as her parents had offered to help pay for the wedding of their only daughter.

She doubted they were expecting something so grand.

'Don't worry.' Juan winked as he watched her lick dry lips. 'We're getting a good discount, given that it's the owners' son's wedding.'

'That's your parents' restaurant?' It was beyond amazing, a huge Parisian-style building, nothing like the corner café she'd been expecting.

'When you said you worked in the café after school…' She'd had visions of young Juan wrapping up kebabs and mopping floors.

'Oh, I meant restaurant,' Juan said, and she remembered then how carefully he had chosen that word.

'Liar!' Cate laughed.

'I was then.' Juan smiled. 'I told no one anything of my past. It is one of the best restaurants in Buenos Aires, perhaps the best. My parents are world-renowned chefs—they hoped I would follow in their footsteps and I thought about it for a while.'

'Oh.' Cate swallowed. 'So that fish that tasted more amazing than I could begin to describe, that marinade…'

'Is my mother's recipe,' Juan explained. 'I didn't go fishing that morning—but I knew I could seduce you with food…' He gave her a nudge. 'As it turned out, I didn't need it.'

'Stop!' Cate blushed at the memory of them in the kitchen.

'Juan is a beautiful cook,' Ramona sighed. 'A waste of your talent…'

They were all mad, all gorgeous and all about to become her family, and then Cate remembered. 'Oh, God! All those meals I've cooked you…'

'What meals?' Juan checked. 'You mean cheese on toast, egg on toast, beans on toast…?' How he teased. 'You do make a nice roast lamb, if a little dry.' He put his arm around her. 'I'm a good catch.'

He looked at her serious hazel eyes and he was certain.

More certain in love than he had ever been.

'And I am so glad that I caught you,' he said.

EPILOGUE

IN CATE'S DREAMS she relived it.

'You look wonderful,' Juan said as he kissed her at the entrance to the church.

Cate had never seen Juan in a suit, and he looked exquisite. He had on a slate-grey tie that matched his eyes and she knew he would have been so grateful for the fingers able to knot it, so grateful for each button on his shirt that he was able to do up. The dawning smile on Juan's face when he saw her wedding dress made her blush. It was a very pale lilac, like the skirt she had worn when he'd first kissed her, and it had a halterneck top—together they smiled at the memories they had already created, in the knowledge there was so much more to come.

'We do this walk together,' Juan's rich voice told her as, with Juan's father and Cate's mother and Eduard behind them, hand in hand they walked down the aisle. And then they faced each other and offered their vows, and Cate needed no translation.

Every word was heartfelt in whatever language it was spoken.

Their future was together, come what may, Cate had

known as a very special ring was moved from her right hand to her left.

Caught between waking and sleeping on her first morning as Juan's wife, she remembered the reception, surrounded by family and new friends. Dancing a terrible tango and drinking *fernet* and cola, then coming back to the hotel.

Cate moaned in her sleep as she recalled their love-making, because if ever there was a bride more inappropriately named it was Mrs Morales!

'Cate?'

She heard her name being called but she didn't want to wake up, didn't want to move away from the bliss of being kissed by him. His tongue mingled with hers and she relished the scent of him, the feel of his hands roaming her body.

Juan checked her finger and the ring was there. He ran a hand along her legs and kissed her until they moved and wrapped tightly around him.

'Cate?'

She heard her name again and moaned as he slid inside her, wanted to be woken like this each and every morning. Her hands slipped up his shoulders and to his neck and he didn't halt her this time. Nothing was out of bounds now. Instead, she opened her eyes to him as together they lived the dream.

* * * * *

Mills & Boon® Hardback
February 2014

ROMANCE

A Bargain with the Enemy	Carole Mortimer
A Secret Until Now	Kim Lawrence
Shamed in the Sands	Sharon Kendrick
Seduction Never Lies	Sara Craven
When Falcone's World Stops Turning	Abby Green
Securing the Greek's Legacy	Julia James
An Exquisite Challenge	Jennifer Hayward
A Debt Paid in Passion	Dani Collins
The Last Guy She Should Call	Joss Wood
No Time Like Mardi Gras	Kimberly Lang
Daring to Trust the Boss	Susan Meier
Rescued by the Millionaire	Cara Colter
Heiress on the Run	Sophie Pembroke
The Summer They Never Forgot	Kandy Shepherd
Trouble On Her Doorstep	Nina Harrington
Romance For Cynics	Nicola Marsh
Melting the Ice Queen's Heart	Amy Ruttan
Resisting Her Ex's Touch	Amber McKenzie

MEDICAL

Tempted by Dr Morales	Carol Marinelli
The Accidental Romeo	Carol Marinelli
The Honourable Army Doc	Emily Forbes
A Doctor to Remember	Joanna Neil

0114GEN STD HB

Mills & Boon® Large Print
February 2014

ROMANCE

The Greek's Marriage Bargain	Sharon Kendrick
An Enticing Debt to Pay	Annie West
The Playboy of Puerto Banús	Carol Marinelli
Marriage Made of Secrets	Maya Blake
Never Underestimate a Caffarelli	Melanie Milburne
The Divorce Party	Jennifer Hayward
A Hint of Scandal	Tara Pammi
Single Dad's Christmas Miracle	Susan Meier
Snowbound with the Soldier	Jennifer Faye
The Redemption of Rico D'Angelo	Michelle Douglas
Blame It on the Champagne	Nina Harrington

HISTORICAL

A Date with Dishonour	Mary Brendan
The Master of Stonegrave Hall	Helen Dickson
Engagement of Convenience	Georgie Lee
Defiant in the Viking's Bed	Joanna Fulford
The Adventurer's Bride	June Francis

MEDICAL

Miracle on Kaimotu Island	Marion Lennox
Always the Hero	Alison Roberts
The Maverick Doctor and Miss Prim	Scarlet Wilson
About That Night...	Scarlet Wilson
Daring to Date Dr Celebrity	Emily Forbes
Resisting the New Doc In Town	Lucy Clark

Mills & Boon® Hardback
March 2014

ROMANCE

A Prize Beyond Jewels	Carole Mortimer
A Queen for the Taking?	Kate Hewitt
Pretender to the Throne	Maisey Yates
An Exception to His Rule	Lindsay Armstrong
The Sheikh's Last Seduction	Jennie Lucas
Enthralled by Moretti	Cathy Williams
The Woman Sent to Tame Him	Victoria Parker
What a Sicilian Husband Wants	Michelle Smart
Waking Up Pregnant	Mira Lyn Kelly
Holiday with a Stranger	Christy McKellen
The Returning Hero	Soraya Lane
Road Trip With the Eligible Bachelor	Michelle Douglas
Safe in the Tycoon's Arms	Jennifer Faye
Awakened By His Touch	Nikki Logan
The Plus-One Agreement	Charlotte Phillips
For His Eyes Only	Liz Fielding
Uncovering Her Secrets	Amalie Berlin
Unlocking the Doctor's Heart	Susanne Hampton

MEDICAL

Waves of Temptation	Marion Lennox
Risk of a Lifetime	Caroline Anderson
To Play with Fire	Tina Beckett
The Dangers of Dating Dr Carvalho	Tina Beckett

Mills & Boon® Large Print
March 2014

ROMANCE

Million Dollar Christmas Proposal	Lucy Monroe
A Dangerous Solace	Lucy Ellis
The Consequences of That Night	Jennie Lucas
Secrets of a Powerful Man	Chantelle Shaw
Never Gamble with a Caffarelli	Melanie Milburne
Visconti's Forgotten Heir	Elizabeth Power
A Touch of Temptation	Tara Pammi
A Little Bit of Holiday Magic	Melissa McClone
A Cadence Creek Christmas	Donna Alward
His Until Midnight	Nikki Logan
The One She Was Warned About	Shoma Narayanan

HISTORICAL

Rumours that Ruined a Lady	Marguerite Kaye
The Major's Guarded Heart	Isabelle Goddard
Highland Heiress	Margaret Moore
Paying the Viking's Price	Michelle Styles
The Highlander's Dangerous Temptation	Terri Brisbin

MEDICAL

The Wife He Never Forgot	Anne Fraser
The Lone Wolf's Craving	Tina Beckett
Sheltered by Her Top-Notch Boss	Joanna Neil
Re-awakening His Shy Nurse	Annie Claydon
A Child to Heal Their Hearts	Dianne Drake
Safe in His Hands	Amy Ruttan

Discover more romance at

www.millsandboon.co.uk

❤ WIN great prizes in our exclusive competitions

❤ BUY new titles before they hit the shops

❤ BROWSE new books and REVIEW your favourites

❤ SAVE on new books with the Mills & Boon® Bookclub™

❤ DISCOVER new authors

PLUS, to chat about your favourite reads, get the latest news and find special offers:

🄵 Find us on facebook.com/millsandboon

🐦 Follow us on twitter.com/millsandboonuk

❤ Sign up to our newsletter at millsandboon.co.uk